cold feet

A Largo Ridge Novel

USA Today Bestselling Author
SAMANTHA A. COLE

Suspenseful Seduction Publishing

one

On a cool, overcast day, Buck Thompson stood between his two best friends, Ryan Vaughn and Justin Haber, in St. Mary's cemetery in Largo Ridge, New Hampshire. It was a place they'd spent far too much time in, grieving over one loss or another during their thirty-plus years on this earth.

Buck's father, both of Ryan's parents, most of their grandparents, a friend from middle school who'd died of cancer, another friend who'd been in a fatal skiing accident, and Noah Scott, their fourth musketeer who'd been killed in Afghanistan, were all buried there. And today, Buck, Ryan, and Justin were there to say goodbye to the man who'd been like a second father to all three of them—Noah's father, Matthew Scott, who'd suffered a massive heart attack less than a week ago.

Mr. Scott had served in the Army in his youth and had lost his right leg in a training accident that'd killed two others in his squad. After receiving a prosthetic leg and a medical discharge, he'd returned to his hometown where he married his high school sweetheart and took over his family's business—the Largo Ridge Ski Resort. Together, he and Grace had made the forty-guest room resort a place where many clients returned year after year. Some of those faithful visitors were now bringing their children and grandchildren on ski vacations like they'd done with their own parents.

Three days after Buck had been born, Mr. & Mrs. Scott had welcomed their only child, a son, into the world. After Noah had started school, he'd become best friends with Buck, Justin, and Ryan. Theirs had been a true brotherhood. Arguments had been few and far between among the four, with most of them being resolved with rock, paper, scissors.

Today, the men were as close as ever, minus Noah. Buck could still remember the phone call he'd received from Ryan to let him know Noah's helicopter had gone down and there'd been no survivors. That was the day Buck had truly understood the word grief. He'd felt like a part of his soul had been ripped from his body. Even now, tears filled his eyes and the sense of loss raced through him as he glanced over at the tombstone at the head of Noah's grave, next to the one that had been dug for today's services.

Sitting on chairs in front of the three friends were Mrs. Scott and her niece, Maxine. Sixteen years ago, the Scotts had taken in the then fourteen-year-old girl after her mother had been arrested and found guilty of murdering a convenience store clerk, along with her drug-addict boyfriend at the time. At least that'd happened in Ohio, so Maxine had been able to start over in Largo Ridge without a scarlet letter on her chest. At the teen's request, her aunt and uncle had arranged to have her name legally changed from Judy Maxine Rhodes to Maxine Scott after she'd come to live with them. Very few people in Largo Ridge knew about Maxi's background, but they included the men she'd come to love as surrogate brothers—her cousin Noah's three best friends. The men would take her secret to the grave, never wanting her to be humiliated by her birth mother's actions—something she'd had no control over.

As the Army honor guard readied for the twenty-one-gun salute, Justin and Ryan both lifted a hand and set them on Buck's shoulders, silently lending their support and, hopefully, keeping him from having a PTSD flashback. He appreciated their concern just as much as he hated it. Combat hadn't been kind to Buck—not that it was ever kind to anyone involved. And now, the sound of gunshots had the power to bring him to his knees or make him take off running in a panic before his mind registered he was no longer in that hellhole a half a world away.

The first of three volleys from the seven rifles had his knees shaking as if an earthquake had rumbled to the surface. The hands on his shoulders squeezed gently, letting him know they were still there. The second volley caused his entire body to break out in a cold sweat under his good suit. When the third round was fired off, he had to swallow back the bile that'd threatened to spew from his mouth.

As "Taps" was played, he pulled a black bandana from his back pocket with a shaking hand and wiped his wet brow and upper lip. After a moment, he nodded his thanks to his two friends. By the time the American flag that'd been draped over the casket had been folded and presented to Mrs. Scott, Buck was back in control of his body and mind again. All three men reached out and touched Mrs. Scott's shoulders and upper arms as she hugged the reminder of her husband's military service. Maxi laid a consoling hand on her aunt's thigh.

After the services concluded, Buck, Justin, and Ryan waited with Mrs. Scott and Maxi while the rest of the mourners placed flowers atop the gray casket and returned to their vehicles. A repast to celebrate Matthew Scott's life was being held at a nearby restaurant, and everyone had been invited.

Once they were the only ones still standing at the grave site, the men helped Mrs. Scott and Maxi to their feet, so they could all say their goodbyes together. A few minutes later, Maxi escorted her aunt to the waiting limousine that would take them to the restaurant, and the three friends headed for Justin's truck.

As they approached the black Chevy Silverado, an older, gray-haired man dressed in a dark suit, stepped in their way, stopping them in their tracks. "Excuse me, gentlemen. My name is Howard Millner—I'm the Scotts' attorney. Forgive me for interrupting your day of mourning, but I wanted to make certain I touched base with you before Mr. Thompson returned to Massachusetts, as per Matthew's orders."

"Orders?" Ryan asked, obviously as confused as Justin and Buck were.

"Yes, you see, Matthew has named all three of you in his will, along with Grace and Maxine. I've already arranged to meet with the ladies on Friday at ten a.m. for the reading of the will. Is that a good time for you all to attend?"

The friends glanced at each other, their confusion deepening. Buck asked what the others were probably thinking, "Why would Mr. Scott put us in his will?"

"I'm afraid I can't disclose that until Friday." He held out three business cards. "Can I expect you at ten?"

Each one took a card before eyeing the others. Ryan and Justin both shrugged and nodded at Buck, who turned back to the lawyer. "I guess we'll all be there."

"I'll see you on Friday then. Take care, gentlemen, and I'm sorry for your loss. Matthew was a good man."

As the man walked away, Buck studied the business card in his hand, hoping it would give him some clue as to what was going on. Unfortunately, that didn't happen.

"Why would he put us in his will?" Justin asked, repeating Buck's earlier question.

Ryan stuffed his card in the pocket of his suit jacket. "Beats me. Should we ask Mrs. Scott?"

Buck shook his head. "No. She's got enough to deal with right now. We'll know in two days. It's probably something small to remember him by."

Pushing his curiosity aside, Buck started for the truck again with the others following. He'd gotten over the worst of the day. Now, it was time to sit back and toast the man they'd loved and respected for most of their lives.

"HE LEFT US WHAT?" Buck burst out as they sat in a conference room in the lawyer's office shortly after 10:00 a.m. on Friday. He glanced at Justin's stunned face, then Ryan's, before settling his wide-eyed gaze on Grace Scott's smile. The sixty-one-year-old woman's dirty-blonde hair had only recently started turning gray. If they'd all been standing, the three men would have towered over her five-foot-two, plump frame, but she could whip them all into shape with just a disapproving look in their direction if they'd been fucking up in some way.

"Don't look so surprised, boys," she said. "Matthew and I had always thought the resort would be passed down to Noah." A flash of sadness crossed her face before she continued. "But, since that wasn't meant to be, we decided to do the next best thing. You boys were and still are our son's best friends. After his death, you always brought him up in conversations with us, remembering all the good times, and making Matthew and I smile and laugh despite our grief. While growing up, I think you spent more time with us at the resort than you did at your own homes some years. You've all worked there during your teens, and even while visiting after you all enlisted, you still had no problem pitching in whenever help was needed. You know that place inside and out. So, Matthew and I decided a few years ago to leave each of you and Maxine a share of the resort. While I'll still have a controlling interest, when I pass on, you'll each inherit an equal share of my ownership."

"Holy sh—" Ryan caught himself before the rest of the expletive rushed out of his mouth. "Sorry."

Justin took a deep breath and let it out slowly. "Mrs. Scott, I don't know what to say."

"First of all," she responded, "I think it's time you all started calling me Grace. After all, you're in your thirties, all grown up and then some, and now, we are also partners. Second, this wasn't a decision Matthew and I made lightly. As I walk around the resort, I always recall images in my mind of the four of you, at different ages, laughing and playing and enjoying life. We wanted that to continue. We wanted you all to start families and raise them the way you were raised—with friends and loved ones. Maxi can't run the resort on her own after I'm gone —she has her practice to deal with." Her niece had gone to school to become a veterinarian and had returned to Largo Ridge to mentor under a local vet after graduation. She'd taken over his practice after he'd retired last year.

Grace continued. "Matthew and I knew we couldn't pass on the resort to anyone but the four of you, but we also understood it might not be what you wanted either. If any of you want to back out, the others will receive your share, and I'll understand. However, if all of you feel this isn't something you want, then I'll start preparing the resort to be listed for sale."

Well, hell. That wasn't something any of them wanted to happen, Buck thought. While they were all still flabbergasted, including Maxi, who hadn't said a word yet, the offer couldn't have come at a better time. Justin and Ryan had both left the military six and seven months ago, respectively, with Justin now working for his brother-in-law's construction company. Ryan had taken over as maintenance supervisor at the resort when Mr.

7

Scott had offered him the job when the previous one had retired a month after Ryan had returned home to Largo Ridge. As for Buck, his honorable discharge had been finalized ten days ago. He was done with the military but hadn't decided what to do as a civilian yet. It looked like Mr. Scott had made that decision for him, and Buck didn't mind one bit.

He sat up straighter in the leather chair next to Ryan. "I'm in."

"Me too," Ryan added. "I work there already anyway."

They both looked at Justin who grinned. "I really hate working for my brother-in-law, so, yeah, I'm in, too."

All eyes flickered to thirty-year-old Maxi. She shook her head, her long, auburn hair swishing across her slender shoulders, but there was amusement in her hazel eyes. "You know, the last thing I ever expected was to be in business with the three of you, but I couldn't ask for better partners. If you all agree I can be a silent partner, helping out when and where I can, then I'm in."

All three men smiled. "Deal."

two

Five months later...
Scarsdale, New York.

"*Y*ou look absolutely beautiful, Gi," Zia Kemp said as she adjusted her best friend's veil.

Regina Vaughn stared at her reflection in the free-standing mirror, that had been brought into the hotel suite, and wished she felt as beautiful as everyone had been saying she looked. All she saw, though, was a bundle of nerves dressed in itchy, white lace and silk and wearing layers of makeup meant to enhance her features. The $12,000 designer dress hadn't been her first choice. In fact, it hadn't even been in her top ten, but she'd been outvoted, so there she stood, in a dress she couldn't wait to take off.

Her heart pounded in her chest as the minutes until she walked down the aisle passed by too quickly for her comfort. This was a mistake. A woman shouldn't be ready to burst into tears on her wedding day for any other reason than she was deliriously happy, right?

All around her, the bridesmaids and mother and aunt of the groom bustled to gather their things. The limos had arrived to take them to the church where Regina's fiancé, Edward Harnett IV, would be waiting for her. He was a sweet man, and she really did love him, but she wasn't *in* love with him. She'd thought she'd been, but if that were true, she wouldn't be dreaming and fantasizing about the man she'd only kissed once several years ago, right? Seriously, what woman dreamed about a man she hadn't seen in what felt like forever instead of the man she was about to marry?

Eleven months ago, the wedding arrangements had quickly blown to epic proportions from the moment Edward had announced to his family that he and Regina had become engaged. With no immediate family in New York, and only a few close friends, Regina had accepted Margaret Harnett's help with everything from the choice of venue, food, flowers, band, dresses, tuxedos, and so much more. It hadn't taken long for Edward's mother, and the wedding planner she'd hired, to simply take over orchestrating the entire event. At first, Regina had been gracious, considering the Harnetts had offered to pay for the grand affair, since her parents had died in a car accident seven years ago. But then, as the months had dragged on, Regina found she'd had no say in most parts of the very expensive wedding, right down to where they'd be spending their honeymoon. She'd always had a hard time saying no to people, and this had been one of the worst experiences of her life due to that personality trait.

None of that was the point though. She couldn't marry a man she wasn't in love with, no matter how much it would hurt him. Edward and his parents would be humiliated in front of three hundred and forty guests, most of them their family, friends, and business associates. Regina's brother, Ryan, was supposed to give her away, and Zia and another close friend, Courtney Fields, were two of her eight bridesmaids. The other six were all from Edward's side of the family—his sister and five cousins, two of whom Regina had met for the first time last night at the rehearsal dinner. She only had about another dozen people included on the guest list. Three cousins she hadn't seen in two years but spoke to occasionally on the phone or via email, and a few other friends who were more than acquaintances but less than BFFs. It'd made her realize how few true friends she had in New York. Zia was the only friend from Largo Ridge, New Hampshire whom Regina had remained friends with after moving to Manhattan to attend Hunter College eight years ago. And that was because Zia had moved there also, to attend NYU.

After getting her bachelor's degree, Regina had applied for and gotten a job with Harnett, Fuller, & Gray, one of the biggest accounting firms in New York City, while also working toward her master's degree. It had helped that she'd been dating Greg Harnett's son for a little over two months at that point.

At first, there'd been a number of people at HF&G

who thought that was the only reason she'd been hired. But it hadn't taken her long to prove her work was on par or better than that of others who'd been there much longer than her. That's not to say there weren't still a few who resented her relationship with Edward.

Regina had met her fiancé one day, completely by accident—literally. The bottom of a bag of groceries she'd been carrying back to her apartment had ripped open and had sent several cans rolling off the sidewalk into the street. Edward had been riding his bicycle and had hit a can of tomatoes, which had caused him to crash into a postal box. Thankfully, he'd been uninjured, save for a few bumps and scratches, but talk about a meet-cute. After listening to Regina say she was sorry for fifteen minutes, he said the only way he'd accept her apology was if she'd agree to have dinner with him at his favorite Italian restaurant the next night. That had ended up being their first date. Twenty-six months later, he was waiting for her at the altar, and she was realizing she couldn't go through with it. Not when Buck Thompson occupied her thoughts more than Edward did.

God, she was such a fool, longing for a man—one of her brother's best friends in the whole world—who didn't want anything to do with her. But that one kiss, seven years ago, when she'd been nineteen, six years his junior, still felt like yesterday. If she closed her eyes and blocked everything else out, she could remember how his lips felt against hers, how he tasted, and how he'd kissed her like he wanted more from her.

It'd been a farce, however. He'd ripped his mouth from

hers, mumbled an apology, then practically ran out the door of her parents' house. For the rest of her summer vacation—three whole weeks—she hadn't seen him again before returning to New York. She'd been in Buck's presence a few times since then—mostly in the days following the fateful morning Dennis and Maria Vaughn's sedan had been hit head-on by a truck driven by a man who'd suffered a diabetic crisis. All three had been killed on impact.

Buck and Ryan's two other best friends, Noah Scott and Justin Haber, along with Zia and Courtney, and their families, had been the Vaughn siblings' rocks during that time. Both in the Army, Justin and Buck had been stateside, stationed in New York and Massachusetts respectively, when the accident had happened, and had managed to return home to Largo Ridge and help Regina until her brother could get there. Ryan and Noah had been in the Marines and stationed in the Middle East at the same time. While Noah had been unable to get leave, like Ryan had, he'd stayed in contact with the others during the whole ordeal. A year after, almost to the day, they'd said their final goodbyes to Regina and Ryan's folks, they'd buried Noah. He'd been killed in a helicopter crash, alongside three other Marines and five Navy SEALs, shortly after taking off from their base in Afghanistan.

That had been a rough year for both Regina and Ryan. She'd been considered a kid sister by all her brother's best friends, and the emotional support had gone both ways as they'd all dealt with their grief in different manners and stages. Between Ryan's financial help and the insurance policy payouts on both their parents and the vehicle, Regina had managed to continue her education at Hunter, however, there hadn't been much left over to pay for a wedding.

"You know," Zia whispered in Regina's ear, so no one else could hear. "There's still time to make a run for it if you change your mind. I'll run interference for you with the groom's mother-zilla over there."

It was as if Zia had read her mind. More than once over the past several months, Regina's best friend had asked if she was certain Edward was the man she wanted to marry. Regina had always said yes but was now regretting the automatic response.

A loud knock at the door to the two-room suite had Regina glancing over her shoulder. When Zia opened the door, Ryan strode in, looking more handsome than ever, wearing a black tuxedo, and receiving lustful stares from several of the bridesmaids, including Courtney. Zia, on the other hand, had always called Ryan a "brother from another mother" and didn't treat him any differently than Regina did.

Despite being six years apart, the Vaughn siblings were very close and even had many of the same facial features. They'd both inherited their mother's blue eyes and their father's mouth, nose, and jet-black hair—Ryan's being short and wavy, while Regina's was long and pin-straight. However, that's where the similarities between them ended. Ryan was six four to Regina's five feet five. He was lean and solid muscle, while she had wide hips and was always trying to lose those pesky fifteen pounds she'd put on during her freshman year at college. Ryan excelled at languages and history and had gone into the military, while she had a mind for numbers and science and had managed to hold a 4.0 GPA every semester at Hunter. He was outgoing and made friends easily. Regina was shy and felt awkward in crowds. Yet, they were as close as they could possibly be, calling and texting each other several times a week, especially now that Ryan had been discharged from the Marines and had returned to Largo Ridge.

After greeting the women in the room, he said, "You all look beautiful, ladies, but not as beautiful as my sister." Through the reflection in the mirror, he winked at Regina. "The limos are waiting for you downstairs, if you could give me a few minutes alone with her."

Margret Harnett patted his arm and smiled. "Of course we will. Just don't be long. We don't want to keep the guests waiting."

"I promise we'll be there on time."

It took about five minutes for everyone to finally clear out of the suite and leave the siblings alone. Ryan stepped over to where Regina still stood in front of the mirror. He glanced down and avoided the dress's train as he sidled in next to her, staring at her reflection. "You really do look beautiful, sis. I know Mom and Dad are smiling down on you right now, saying the same thing."

His words opened the floodgates holding back her tears. Her lips trembled as drops rolled down her cheeks. A sob was ripped from her chest as Ryan grasped her shoulders and turned her toward him. "Crap, Gi, what's wrong?" When she just cried harder, he continued. "Baby, this is supposed to be the happiest day of your life, but I don't think these are happy tears. Tell me."

She tilted her head back so she could see his face which was filled with concern and confusion. "I-I can't do it, Ry. I can't marry Edward."

Confusion morphed to anger on his handsome face. "What did he do to you?"

"No-nothing, I swear. He's really a nice guy. I-I just know if we get married today, it'll be the biggest m-mistake of my life."

Pulling her into his arms, he held her tightly against his chest as she bawled her eyes out. He didn't seem to care that her allegedly water-proof mascara was staining his crisp, white shirt—not that it was his, because it came with the rented tuxedo. "This isn't just a case of cold feet, is it? You're not going to regret it if you don't get married, right?"

"No. I-I'll regret it if I do. I love him, Ry, but I'm not *in* love with him. I want what Mom and Dad had, and I don't see that ever happening between Edward and me."

She felt his light chuckle through his chest. "They did have a grand love affair, didn't they? I remember being embarrassed as a kid because they danced, held hands, and always looked at each other like no one else was in the room. That was true love. In a weird way, I'm grateful they died together. I know it felt like hell to both of us, but I honestly couldn't see either of them surviving without the other for long." He pulled back just enough so he could peer down at her face. "If you know in your heart getting married to Edward isn't right for you, I'll drive the getaway car."

Through watery eyes, a small smile lit up her face. "I knew I could count on you, big brother. I can't face Edward and his parents and friends right now." She snorted. "Hell, I probably won't have a job at his father's company after today either. Take me home to Largo Ridge, please? At least there, I'll be able to think about what I'm going to do next."

"Do we need to swing by your apartment for some clothes and stuff?"

Regina shook her head. Most of her things were packed in boxes in the apartment she'd shared with Courtney and Zia. Edward's mother hadn't approved of Regina moving in with him until after the wedding. Movers had been scheduled to transfer her stuff to Edward's brownstone the day after they returned from their honeymoon. "No, I have enough in the suitcases here in the bedroom. We were leaving for the airport first thing after breakfast tomorrow. And you know me, I overpacked. I also have some warmer clothes at the house I left there last time I was home."

Home. Now that she said that word in reference to Largo Ridge, she finally realized New York had never felt like home to her—not the way the snowy mountains in New Hampshire did. She missed Largo Ridge, her brother, and the friends she'd let drift away after she'd moved south. She missed the quiet of the peaceful nights when you could see more stars in the heavens than you could count in a lifetime.

There was something other than all those things that she missed as well—more like someone—but she was too upset and disorientated at the moment to admit that to

17

herself. For now, she'd let Ryan take her home. Once they were in the car, she'd call Zia and ask her to tell Edward she wasn't coming. Her best friend would do that for her, no questions asked until later. Hopefully, by then, Regina would have some answers for her.

three

Six months later . . .

"*Here* you go," Zia said, setting a large Bloody Mary next to Regina's laptop at the kitchen table in the house the Vaughn siblings had grown up in. "Drink that before you have a conniption. I doubled the amount of vodka I usually put in, figuring you'd need it."

Still in shock, Regina stared at the engagement announcement on the website of *The New York Times*.

> *Mr. & Mrs. Robert Fields announce the engagement of their daughter, Courtney, to Edward J. Harnett IV, son of Mr. & Mrs. Edward J. Harnett III . . .*

She couldn't believe it . . . actually, on second thought, yes, she could.

On what had supposed to have been her wedding day, it'd taken Regina only a few minutes to get out of the dress she'd so hated and change into a pair of jeans, a T-shirt, and sneakers. Then she'd called Zia and told her the wedding was off. Her friend had sounded more relieved than shocked and in a hushed voice had said she would break the news to Edward as soon as the limo she was in arrived at the church.

Regina had left the dress in the suite, along with her veil and shoes, Ryan's tuxedo he'd changed out of, and nothing more. She should have written Edward a note or something, but she'd needed time to think about what to say, and she and Ryan had wanted to be out of the hotel before all hell broke loose.

Seven minutes after Ryan had bundled her and both of their suitcases into his truck and given the waiting limo driver a huge tip for the canceled ride, they'd merged into traffic on the northbound Hutchinson River Parkway. A minute later, Regina's phone had blown up with calls and text messages. Unable to summon the courage to talk to Edward yet, she'd turned off her phone after shooting off a text to tell Zia to call Ryan if she needed her.

Not long after they'd crossed over the New York/Connecticut border, Regina had remembered she'd still been wearing her engagement ring and the antique pearl earrings Edward's grandmother had loaned her for her "something old." Removing them, she'd stuck the jewelry in her purse until she could send them back to Edward via certified mail. Even if she'd thought about it back at the hotel, it wouldn't have been a good idea to leave the two-and-a-half-carat diamond ring and heirloom earrings unattended in the suite.

Without the heavy rock on her hand, it'd felt like a weight had also been lifted off her shoulders. How she'd let the engagement go on for as long as it had would always be a mystery to her.

Little had been said during the five-hour drive to Largo Ridge, and Regina had been grateful her brother hadn't pushed her into any conversations. Instead, they'd listened to the radio and had only spoken when necessary. She knew he hadn't been mad at her. In fact, he'd reached over a few times and squeezed her shoulder or hand in silent support. Thank goodness she'd been blessed with such a wonderful older brother.

After they'd entered Largo Ridge's town limits, instead of the champagne and Chateaubriand that would've been served at the Harnett's country club, where the reception was supposed to have been held, Regina and Ryan had agreed on takeout. A pepperoni pie from the famous—locally—Say Cheez Pizzeria and a six-pack of Budweiser had been just what Regina had needed. Well, that and a lot of sleep, which she hadn't been able to get the night before.

The next day, she'd finally bitten the bullet and called Edward. It hadn't been a pleasant conversation. She'd been right—he and his parents had been humiliated in front of their family, friends, and business associates. Regina had cried through most of the phone call, but when it had finally ended, she knew she'd made the right decision to cancel the wedding. Edward had been more upset about the forfeited money for the reception, his reputation, and his parents' anger than he'd been about losing her.

Ten days later, Ryan, Justin, and Buck had driven back to Manhattan with Regina to help her pack up her things.

She'd canceled the movers who'd been supposed to take everything to Edward's place. Thankfully, her brother's friends had given her the front passenger seat for the round trip, so she'd been able to ignore Buck for the most part. Zia had taken the day off work, and between the five of them, they'd filled the small U-Haul trailer attached to Ryan's truck in under two hours. Regina had been a little surprised when Courtney hadn't come home straight from work to say goodbye to her. The two of them had become friends at Hunter College, and Regina had invited Courtney to move in with her and Zia when they'd been looking for an apartment to share.

During the first few days after the wedding fiasco, Regina had talked to Courtney almost as much as she'd talked to Zia over the phone. But then their calls had become less frequent and shorter until they were nonexistent. A month later, Zia had told Regina the reason why—Courtney had not only been talking to Regina but also with Edward. The next thing they knew, Courtney and Edward had started dating. Clearly, it'd been a whirlwind romance, since they were now engaged.

Knowing the announcement was going to be in today's Sunday edition of NYC's largest newspaper, Zia had rented a car for the weekend and come home to Largo Ridge to be there when Regina found out about Courtney's betrayal.

Now, sitting across the table from her best friend, Zia took a long pull on the straw in her own Bloody Mary. "Ah . . . perfection." She stared at Regina a moment. "You know, I never really cared for her. If it wasn't for you, she and I would never have been anything more than acquaintances. And it doesn't surprise me she went after Edward. She was always jealous of you and him—and I'm sure she's only marrying him for his money. Well, his parents' money."

"Really? I always thought she was nice. I mean, we had fun together."

"You always see the good in people, Gi. You really need to learn to take a closer look at them. Not everyone is as nice as you think they are."

"It's better than being cynical," she retorted without any heat.

"Is it?"

Was Zia right? Had Regina really been that blind not to see Courtney's friendship hadn't been true? Well, it didn't matter now, did it? She hadn't spoken to Courtney in months and probably never would again. It was time to move on and not stress over the past.

Picking up her glass, she lifted it toward Zia. "To the happy couple. Better her than me."

Zia clinked their glasses together. "Here, here."

"What're we celebrating?" Ryan asked as he strode into the kitchen with Buck on his heels just as Regina was taking another sip of her drink. During Ryan's and his friends' military careers, they'd learned how to walk into a place without making a sound. He'd scared the crap out of her more than once since she'd been living with him again—most of the time, it'd been unintentional.

At the sight of the man she'd had an erotic dream about last night—again—she sucked too hard on the straw and the liquid splashed against the back of her throat, causing her to choke and sputter. She snatched a napkin from the holder on the table and pressed it to her mouth to keep from spewing red everywhere. Her eyes watered as she tried to pull oxygen into her lungs instead of tomato juice, horseradish, vodka, and whatever else Zia had put in the mix.

"Are you okay, squirt?" The nickname Buck had given her, when she'd been around five or six, barely registered in her mind, as she struggled to get her trachea and lungs working again. Buck had a smug look on his face and a twinkle in his beautiful, amber eyes, as if he knew the reason for her nearly choking to death had been because of his presence. *Bastard.*

As soon as she nodded and hoarsely rasped, "Yes," the amusement faded from his ruggedly handsome face as if he'd remembered they'd hardly spoken to each other since that hot kiss they'd shared years ago. His gaze left her face, and he slapped Ryan on the shoulder. "I'll grab the tools from the basement."

"Yeah, go ahead," her brother responded absentmindedly as he started reading the wedding announcement page that was still up on Regina's laptop, while Buck headed for the basement door in the hallway outside the kitchen. "Son of a bitch. Is this for real?"

"Ah-yup." As she spoke, Zia stood, stepped over to the counter, and retrieved another glass from a cabinet. She filled it up with cold water and handed it to Regina. "Gi dodged a bullet it seems. I wonder what the Harnetts' friends and business associates think about getting two wedding invitations in less than a year for the same groom."

"That he's an asshole."

After a few more coughs, Regina managed to take a few sips of the cool water and was grateful when they went down the right pipe. Her eyes kept shifting to the hall doorway as she waited for Buck to return. As much as she hated to admit it, she loved ogling the man—at least when he didn't realize it. He was six two, with broad shoulders, and strong arms and legs. With his short, brown hair, firm jaw, and those amazing eyes she saw in her dreams, the man could easily grace any cover of the many romance books she read each month. And those things were another reason why she should've realized something had been missing between her and Edward. Not that all those books were based on reality—some were far-fetched—but a common theme was the acute chemistry between the main love interests. Sex had been okay with Edward, and in that lay one of the problems. It'd just been okay—nothing that'd resulted in her toes curling or had made her forget her name. And she knew those things could happen with the right man. In fact, they *had* happened . . . with just one kiss from Buck.

BUCK LEANED against the workbench in the Vaughns' basement, willing his cock to behave. The damn thing reacted every time Regina was in view, and today had been no exception. Ryan had wanted to stop by his house to pick up some tools on the way back from town. They'd loaded Ryan's pickup truck with sheets of drywall and were on their way to the fixer-upper farmhouse Buck had bought last month. Try as he might, Buck hadn't been able to give the man an excuse not to. He couldn't come out and say he'd been lusting after his best friend's sister for the past seven years and got a woody every time he saw her. Yeah, that wouldn't have gone over well, especially since Ryan had been in major-protection mode with Regina since bringing the runaway bride home six months ago.

Hadn't that been a kick? Buck should've been elated when Ryan had announced Regina had gotten engaged. Instead, he'd had to hide how jealous and pissed off he'd been and pretend he was happy for her. Thank God she hadn't invited him or Justin to the wedding, probably since they hadn't seen her at all in over two years. Maybe she hadn't wanted to rub her wedding in his face, although she should have.

Around 8:00 a.m. the day after the nuptials had been supposed to have taken place, Buck had been shocked to run into Ryan at a local bagel shop. As far as Buck had known, his friend hadn't planned on returning to Largo Ridge until that evening, hours after Regina had left on her honeymoon. When he'd learned the bride-to-be had canceled the wedding, the triumph Buck had felt had overwhelmed him. He was a bastard thinking that if he couldn't have her, no other man should either.

The shuffling of feet and the scraping of a chair across the tile above his head had Buck returning to the task at hand. Sundays and evenings were the only time he'd been able to devote to working on the farmhouse. There were too many things that had to be done at the ski resort to get it ready for the snow season, which started in a few weeks. While the structure, roof, and foundation of the fifty-year-old house were sound, it'd needed some major updating to the interior and exterior. Since they were getting an early frost this year, the outside of the house would have to wait until the spring for a new paint job and repairs to sections of the wraparound porch. As for the inside, Buck had been tearing down the moldy and damaged walls and ceilings and replacing the old insulation before putting up new drywall. Once that was all done, he'd concentrate on remodeling the kitchen and two baths and stripping and refinishing the wooden floors. Ryan, Justin, and a few other friends had been helping out whenever they could in exchange for a few cases of beer and lunch or dinner or both. Despite not living in Largo Ridge for the past fifteen years, Buck had stayed in touch with many of his friends thanks to the wonders of social media. He'd even been able to return home to see a few of them get married, and now, those friends were posting photos of their kids on Facebook and Instagram. Where had the time flown?

Buck doubted he'd ever get married and have kids. Hell, he wouldn't even spend a whole night with any of the women he dated or had one-night stands with, afraid of hurting them during one of the nightmares his PTSD conjured up on a frequent basis. He couldn't risk it. And it wasn't as if he'd hooked up a lot, but when he had, he'd made sure it was with women who weren't looking for anything more than a good time with a man who could satisfy them in bed. Unfortunately, none of those women ended up in his erotic dreams—only one was front and center every time—Regina, who was too good for him. While her engagement hadn't worked out, someday she'd find a guy she'd be willing to settle down with. What sucked was she'd probably do that with someone from Largo Ridge or one of its surrounding small towns, which meant he'd occasionally have to see her with her husband. At least if she'd married that Edward guy, they would've lived in New York City, and Buck would only run into her once every few years.

Sighing, he selected the tools he and Ryan would need, which Buck hadn't gotten around to adding to his own basement workshop yet, then climbed the stairs, shutting off the overhead light when he reached the top. As he closed the door behind him, Ryan entered the hallway. "Got everything?"

"Yup." He glanced over his friend's shoulder and wasn't sure if he was disappointed or relieved he couldn't see Regina in the kitchen. "Let's get back to my place and unload your truck."

"Sounds good. See you later, ladies!"

"Bye," they responded in chorus from the kitchen.

As Buck strode out of the house, with Ryan right behind him, he called himself ten kinds of a fool for wanting the one woman he couldn't . . . shouldn't have.

four

"Regina! Come on in!"

Carrying her buttery-soft, brown, leather briefcase Ryan had given her when she'd graduated college, Regina smiled as she strode into Grace Scott's office at the resort. So far, so good—she'd made it from the parking lot, through the public areas of the inn, and into the private quarters and hadn't run into Buck.

Shortly after returning to Largo Ridge, she'd been hired by Carney & Brewer CPAs, who handled the books for the ski resort. At Grace's request, Regina had taken over the LRSR's account, and she'd been stopping by every other week to go over the bank deposits, purchase debits, and credit card receipts with the woman. Once a month, she also had to sit down with the other four shareholders to go over the bottom line of the accounts. However, since that'd happened last Tuesday, she had three more weeks before she had to be in the same room with Buck, with no excuse to escape.

Regina had been surprised when she'd been given the

account, but as Grace had explained, she didn't care for Marty Sims, the previous CPA assigned to her, and wanted someone she knew and trusted to take over. Marty had always dealt with Matthew who, in turn, filled his wife in when she wasn't busy with all the things she did around the resort, guaranteeing their guests were comfortable and happy. When Grace had needed to take over the financial aspect of running the place, Marty had apparently talked to the woman as if she didn't have a clue how to balance a checkbook or make change for ten dollars. His misogynistic attitude had rubbed her the wrong way, which was understandable. When she'd learned Regina had been hired by Carney & Brewer, she'd immediately requested her to replace the chauvinistic jackass—her words.

After giving the older woman a hug and a kiss on the cheek, Regina took a seat at the room's small conference table where they could spread out the books and paperwork they needed to go over. She pulled her laptop out of her briefcase and booted it up.

"So, how's everything going?" Grace asked as she joined her at the table, setting a bottle of water next to her and keeping one for herself. She always had them ready before Regina arrived.

The question wasn't about business. Instead, as usual, the woman wanted to know how things were in Regina's personal life before their conversation turned to all things related to LRSR. While she hadn't been as close to the Scotts growing up as Ryan had been, Regina still felt like family around them. Her parents had been friends of the other couple, and the Scotts often attended barbecues and parties at the Vaughns', and they were invited to join any festivities held at the resort.

Regina had felt awful she hadn't been able to return home for Matthew Scott's funeral, but at the time, she'd been involved with an audit for one of Harnett, Fuller, & Gray's most important accounts. Although still being a newbie, she hadn't been in charge of anything. However, it wouldn't have looked good for anyone on that auditing team to take time off for any reason, if they ever wanted to advance in the company. Instead, she'd asked Ryan to add her name to whatever floral display he was sending to the funeral home. Then she'd sent a plant and Mass card to Grace a few days after the services to let her know she was thinking of the new widow. Grace had placed the plant in her office, where it was thriving and had needed to be repotted twice because of its size.

"Good, I guess." Regina took a sip of the water. "I finally unpacked the last of the moving boxes. Can't believe it took me six months to do it." Thankfully, all her wedding shower gifts had been stored in a spare bedroom at Edward's brownstone, otherwise she would've had twice as much stuff. She could only assume the presents had been returned to the shower guests by her former fiancé and his parents. The only gifts that'd been at her apartment had been the ones that Zia and Courtney had given her, and the latter's had been missing when Regina had moved out. During a phone call with Courtney, she'd learned the woman had returned the gift for a refund, seeing how Regina hadn't gone through with the wedding. That should've been Regina's first clue about how their friendship was going to end. Zia, however, had insisted that her best friend keep the trousseau she'd given her, telling her to save the white silk negligee and black, lacy lingerie for when she met Mister Right, since Edward had been Mr. Wrong.

"Well, at least it's finally done. How's the book club you joined? What's on this week's reading list?"

Her eyes lit up. She'd recently run into an old friend from high school, who'd invited her to join her book club after they'd caught up on what each other had been doing since graduation. "Alessandra Torre's new book. I was up late last night reading it and kept telling myself I'd turn off the light after one more chapter. It's fantastic—I'll give it to you when I'm done." Grace was as big a fan of romance novels as Regina was, and both preferred print copies over e-books when it came to their favorite authors.

"Wonderful. Thank you."

"Of course." It wouldn't be the first time they'd swapped books.

Regina clicked on the accounting program to open it on her laptop and then picked up the folder that held the most recent receipts for the resort. "Okay, let's see what we've got here."

Forty-five minutes later, Regina exited the office with her briefcase in hand. After taking over LRSR's account, she'd transferred all the data into a better and more advanced program than the one Marty had been using. Apparently, the man was resistant to change when it came to new ways of doing things.

After deciding to take a chance that she wouldn't run into Buck, Regina detoured on her way out to the parking lot and stepped into the little cafe next to the lobby. They had the best cappuccinos there, and she also bought herself an orange and cranberry scone because they looked delicious.

Needing to get back to the office, she carried her treats out to the parking lot. The crisp mountain air felt like heaven in her lungs. How she'd stayed so long in the smog-filled city was beyond her. She guessed that old saying was true—you don't know what you've got till it's gone.

Regina was almost to her SUV when a male voice shouted her name from somewhere behind her. She stopped short, recognizing Buck's deep timbre immediately. Clearly, she'd been spotted and had heard him, so there was nothing she could do but turn around and face him. Hopefully, whatever he wanted could be taken care of in a second or two, so she could hightail it out of there.

Taking a deep breath, and shoring up her defenses, she spun around. Buck was striding toward her with another man she recognized, but she was drawing a blank on his name. The tall, dark-haired man was one of Buck and Ryan's high school friends, but Regina hadn't known him well and hadn't seen him in years. She hoped Buck would introduce them, so she didn't look like an idiot for not remembering the man's name.

She tried to plaster a friendly smile on her face as they approached her. It wasn't easy to do with Buck's intense gaze on her. "Gi, I don't know if you remember him, but this is Hogan Greer—he went to school with us." He glanced at Hogan. "This is Ryan's kid sister, Regina, but everyone calls her Gi."

Her face fell when he'd referred to her as "Ryan's kid sister," but she recovered quickly before both men looked at her again. Hogan held out his hand. "Nice to meet you. I'm sorry, but I don't remember you from school."

She shook his hand—a working man's hand, strong and rough with callouses but still gentle. He was good-looking too but not as handsome as Buck. And it annoyed her that she thought that. "No worries. I'm six years younger than Ryan, so I wasn't in high school at the same time as you. And honestly, you looked slightly familiar, but I couldn't remember your name. So, I guess that makes us even."

He chuckled. "Okay, that works for me. Um . . . I hope we're not holding you up, but Buck said you're a certified accountant, and I am in desperate need of one. I mean, not for me, personally, but for my nonprofit organization. I've been a wildlife rehabilitation expert with the New Hampshire Fish and Game Department for years, but I just established a new wildlife sanctuary in Largo Ridge, thanks to some very generous donors. Buck says you're great at what you do, so I'd like to hire you to get me set up with everything I need for handling taxes, and then stay on as my accountant afterward, if that's okay."

Buck had said she was great at what she did? Really? Wow. "Um . . . yes, I'd be happy to."

"Do we have to go through the company you're with or can you take this on as a side job? Honestly, if you're doing all the work, I'd rather pay you directly, instead of the company taking a cut. Of course, it's up to you—whichever works."

"Hogan doesn't like corporations," Buck said with a smirk, and his friend snorted then nodded in agreement.

"Well, I'm allowed to take individual clients or non-profits as side jobs, just not businesses, so I most certainly can take you on. Of course, I'll only be able to discuss business with you during the evenings and weekends though."

Hogan held out his hand to her again. "That's fine with me. I have more than enough stuff to do to fill my workweek. Can we get together this Saturday? If you don't mind coming out to the sanctuary, I can show you around and then go over the finances and goals of the organization. I'll even introduce you to Bonnie and Clyde."

Her eyebrows shot up as she shook his hand. "And they would be?"

"I'm raising one-year-old, black bear cubs—siblings—that were orphaned a few months ago. When their mother was hit by a car and killed, they were too young to be rehabilitated back into the wild, so I adopted them. It's how the sanctuary went from being a dream of mine to a reality."

"Seriously? Wow." Sure, she'd seen bears occasionally over the years, wandering around Largo Ridge, searching for food. But like most natives of the area, she gave them a wide berth and made sure not to leave out anything that would attract them. "Um, as long as you promise I won't become dinner for them, I'd love to meet them. Saturday is fine. Around ten?"

SAMANTHA A. COLE

"Perfect." He pulled his cell phone out of his pocket. "What's your phone number? I'll send you a text on Friday to confirm our meeting and give you directions to the sanctuary. It doesn't show up on most GPS devices yet."

She rattled off her cell number and seconds later her phone rang in her jacket pocket. As she took it out and silenced it, Hogan said, "Now you have my number too. Call me if you need to change the time or day, otherwise I'll see you on Saturday."

"Sounds good. And thank you for the job opportunity."

A huge smile showed off his dimples. "And thank you for taking it." He slapped Buck on the shoulder. "Thanks, man. I'll talk to you later."

"Yup."

Hogan strode away, leaving Regina alone with Buck, and she realized it was the first time they'd been close enough to have a conversation, with no one else around, since she'd returned to Largo Ridge. As much as it disconcerted her, she forced herself not to jump into her vehicle and leave. It would be rude not to express her gratitude for him introducing her to Hogan and suggesting the man hire her. "Thank you for recommending me."

With his gaze shifting to the ground, he shrugged and kicked a small pebble to the side. "Ryan mentioned you eventually want to start your own CPA firm. I figured this would give you a step in that direction."

"Well, I really appreciate it."

"Sure."

His gaze returned to her face, and she was surprised to see heat in his stare. It froze her in place for a few moments, but then she remembered the humiliation she'd felt when he'd run from her after their one and only kiss. She gestured toward her SUV. "Um, I have to get back to work. Thanks again."

When she pivoted, he said, "Gi . . ."

Swallowing hard, she glanced back at him. His mouth was open as if he'd wanted to say something but had stopped. After a moment, he shook his head. "I . . . uh . . . never mind. I mean, you're welcome. I'll see you around."

With a half-hearted wave, Buck spun on his heel and walked away. Regina hated that she stood there and watched until he disappeared through the front door of the inn.

five

*S*ighing, Regina hit a button on the remote, shuffling through the channels searching for something to watch that would hold her attention for more than a few minutes. One would think on a Friday night there would be something good on TV, but alas, she couldn't find anything. She had the house to herself for the weekend—Ryan had left that morning for Pennsylvania, where he'd be until Sunday. A guy from his old platoon was getting married and had invited Ryan and a few other Marines they'd served with.

While it was a comfort to be back in her childhood home again, it was also a pain in the ass to be living with her brother sometimes. He was far too noisy when he got up in the morning, a full hour and a half before Regina needed to start her day. They argued over dishes left in the sink, wet towels on the floor of the bathroom, and whose turn it was to vacuum. At that point in her life, Regina had expected to be doing those things with a husband, not her brother.

Although she wanted to get a place of her own, she'd decided to wait until the new year. By then she would have saved up money for all the furniture she'd need. Back in New York, the apartment had been filled with new furniture Zia's rich grandmother had splurged on for them. Sadie Kemp had been widowed for thirty years and had inherited a healthy sum of money from her husband's family. She'd invested it well and had made generous donations to several charities. Her motto among her close family and friends had become, "I can't take it with me, so please let me treat you, just this one time." Of course, "one time" turned into two or three or a dozen for those she loved the most, and her favorite granddaughter was included on that list.

So, now that she was thinking about getting her own place, Regina would need to buy furniture for every room except her bedroom. She'd be able to take a few assorted pieces that were scattered about the Vaughn home, including the attic. Ryan had told her she was welcome to take anything she wanted, since everything belonged to her as much as him, but she couldn't take it all. The house was still in both their names and only had a small mortgage left on it, which Ryan had been paying off with his military and subsequent civilian pay. The least she could do was not steal all his furniture.

As the shows flipped by on the screen, she mentally went over her list of things she was bringing with her to the White Mountain Wildlife Rehabilitation Center and what she had to cover with Hogan. She'd done a little research on the man. He'd graduated from the University of Vermont with a bachelor's in wildlife biology and then had gone on to get his master's in wildlife science. After that, he'd spent the past ten years working for the New Hampshire Fish and Game Department as a wildlife rehabilitation expert, as he'd told her. Recently, the local newspaper had done an article on him and his rescued cubs—Bonnie and Clyde. The photo of him horsing around with the bears had been adorable, although they weren't exactly small anymore. Their plight of being orphans, with Hogan unable to find a zoo or sanctuary that'd been able to take the siblings at the time, had apparently caught the attention of several conservationists. With their support and donations, Hogan had been able to start the White Mountain Wildlife sanctuary. In addition to the bears, he'd taken in a few other injured or orphaned animals, some of which had been able to return to the wild when they'd been healthy enough. A huge enclosure, with trees, boulders, man-made caves, and a waterfall flowing into a pool, was in the process of being built for Bonnie and Clyde, and Regina was looking forward to seeing it and the rest of the sanctuary.

Frustrated and bored, Regina began to scroll through the cable guide for a third time, hoping something would've changed in the last minute or so and a movie or show would catch her eye. She was about to settle on a rerun of *Law & Order* when she heard an explosion in the distance and the house went dark.

She froze.

Oh no, no, no. With the moon behind some clouds, she could barely see her own hand in front of her face. A glance out the living room window revealed the three other houses in their small neighborhood were also dark. Feeling around on the couch next to her, she found her cell phone. She quickly brought it to life and activated the flashlight app. The room lit up, but it didn't slow her pounding heart and increased breathing. A shiver of panic slid down her spine, and she struggled to keep it at bay. The last thing she needed right now was to start hyperventilating.

Due to an incident when she'd been eight years old, she hated the dark. Zia had been visiting, and the two girls had been playing hide and seek. When it was Regina's turn to hide, she'd crawled into the antique hope chest in her parents' bedroom. It'd been empty because her mother had recently inherited the piece of furniture after Regina's great-grandmother had passed away. Her folks had been in the backyard, working on the vegetable garden in a greenhouse her father had built. Ryan and his friends had also been outside, tossing a baseball around, getting ready for a Little League game. Knowing her friend wasn't supposed to be in her parents' bedroom without their permission, Zia hadn't looked in there. Instead, she'd searched the other three bedrooms and the hall bath on the second floor before descending the stairs to try to find her friend somewhere else in the house.

In the meantime, the outside latch on the hope chest had fallen back into place, locking Regina in. When she'd realized the lid wouldn't lift, she'd gotten scared. At first, she was afraid to call out because she didn't want to get into trouble for being in her parents' room. But then panic had set in, and she'd started to cry and scream as she struggled against the lid and walls of the chest. Finally,

Ryan and Buck had come back inside with Zia to help her find her friend and had heard her screeching. Regina had been bruised all over from kicking, punching, and banging her head, and her fingers had been bloody from trying to claw her way out. She'd been inconsolable when they'd rescued her, and it'd taken her mother about an hour to calm her down.

Ever since then, Regina had slept with a digital clock in her room to provide just enough light for her to see if she woke up in the middle of the night. First her mother, and then Regina as she'd gotten older, had always made sure there were fresh batteries in the clock just in case the power went out.

Taking a few deep breaths, she tried to keep her panic in check. Standing on shaky legs, she used the flashlight to make her way into the kitchen where she retrieved a lighter from the utility drawer. There were several scented candles she'd put around the house after she'd moved back in, and she began to light them, praying the power wouldn't be out for too long.

After lighting one in the kitchen and another in the dining room, she returned to the living room. She'd just lit one of two candles on the coffee table when there was a pounding on the front door. She yelped loudly as her heart felt like it would explode from under her ribs. Fear ruling her body, Regina stood frozen in place.

The doorknob rattled. "Gi! It's me! I'm coming in!"

Relief surged through her as the front door swung open, and Buck strode in, his alert gaze taking in the situation. As he kicked the door shut, her knees began to buckle, and he rushed forward and scooped her up in his arms before she could hit the floor. "Shh. I got you, baby."

Holding her tightly, he sat on the couch and settled her on his lap. "I've got you, Gi," he murmured in a soft but reassuring tone. "Everything's going to be fine."

Regina gulped in mouthfuls of air as her body shuddered. Buck's strong arms wrapped around her, and one hand stroked her hair. "It's okay, baby. It's okay."

As much as she hated to admit it, there was no other place she'd rather be, at that very moment, than in Buck Thompson's arms. Soon, she'd have to pull herself together and get off his lap, but for now, she'd let him take care of her and calm her. And hopefully, later, she'd be able to forget about how her body started to respond to his.

six

$\mathcal{R}$eaching behind him, Buck grabbed a blue afghan, that Regina's mother had knitted years ago, from the back of the couch and wrapped it around the scared woman in his lap. She still hadn't stopped shaking, but he knew what would help. After sliding her off his lap, onto the cushion beside him, he stood. "I'll be right back. Okay?" When she didn't look up or answer him, he cupped her chin and lifted until her navy-blue eyes met his brown ones. "Gi? I'm just going into the kitchen, okay? I'll be right back."

Finally, she nodded. Damn, with her wide eyes, pale skin, and trembling lips, she looked years younger. Not wanting to leave her for long, Buck hurried into the kitchen and retrieved two tumblers from one cabinet and a full bottle of Southern Comfort from another. After pouring a few ounces of the amber liquor into each glass, he carried them out to the living room where he found her trying to light a second candle on the coffee table. However, her hands were shaking so badly the flame at the end of the long lighter kept going out. Putting the glasses down, he reached for the lighter. "Here, let me get that."

As he lit the candle for her, she pulled the blanket tighter around her body and sat back on the couch. Taking a seat next to her, he picked up the two glasses again and handed her one. When the whiskey sloshed over the rim, he put his hand over hers and helped her get the glass to her mouth without spilling any more. "Ryan would have a fit if he saw you waste his SoCo like that."

She snorted then took a few sips. He waited patiently as, over the next few minutes, she emptied the glass. "Feel better?"

Nodding, she pulled up her feet and sat cross-legged. While there was still a slight tremor in her hands, the rest of her muscles seemed to be under control. Picking up the other glass, he took a sip and got comfortable.

"What happened? Why did the lights go out and . . . and why are you here?" she asked, albeit hesitantly.

"I was late getting out of work and was about a half mile up the road when I saw and heard an explosion. I have a scanner in my truck that picks up the police, fire, and EMS dispatchers. Apparently, a transformer blew. The fire department and electric company are responding. The power might be out until the morning though. It'll take them a few hours to get a new transformer up and working."

"Thank God." At his surprised look, she shook her head. "I don't mean thank God that the power will be out all night, because that really sucks. I meant thank God it was a transformer that blew and wasn't anything else where someone could've been hurt or killed." She paused. "So, why did you come here?"

He swallowed another sip of the SoCo. "I knew Ryan was away for the weekend and assumed you were home alone. I knew if the power was out, there was a good chance you'd be freaking. I just wanted to check and make sure you were all right."

In the candlelight, he was just able to make out a blush staining her face. "Thanks," she murmured.

Reaching out, he brushed his knuckles against her cheek. "There's nothing to be embarrassed about, Gi."

"Says the man who's not afraid of the dark."

Setting the glass on the coffee table, he turned his body to face her. "Hey, there's nothing wrong with having a phobia after a traumatic event like you had."

"That happened when I was eight, Buck. I'm twenty-six, almost twenty-seven. I shouldn't still be a chickenshit when the lights go out."

"You're not a chickenshit. Everyone has a phobia about at least one thing or another—yours just happens to be of the dark, and you have a damn good reason for having it. Don't be too hard on yourself. Look at Zia—she's afraid of clowns. And your brother—still scared of needles, right?"

She chuckled. "Yup." They sat in silence for a moment, then Regina stood. At Buck's questioning gaze, she said, "If we're going to sit here, in the candlelight, talking without anyone else around for the first time in years— well, second if you count the parking lot the other day— I'm going to owe Ry a bottle of SoCo."

Well, at least she wasn't kicking him out the door. As much as he knew she deserved far better than him, he missed their friendship. Even though she was a few years younger than her brother and his friends, their families had always been close. Maybe with them both living in Largo Ridge again, seeing each other more often, and with a little time, they could get back to where they'd been before he'd been stupid enough to kiss her. He knew he'd hurt her back then, running out on her and leaving her standing there well-kissed but confused, but he'd crossed a line. Ryan was like a brother to him, so that should've made Regina like a sister, right? But a guy didn't have the types of fantasies Buck had about a sister. After all those years, telling himself he'd been an ass for taking advantage of the moment and her naivety, he was still attracted to her. His sweet "squirt" had grown up to become a beautiful woman. One who had guys' heads turning and their tongues and dicks wagging after her. On top of that, she was smart, funny, and caring.

And Buck was damaged goods. He could be friends with her but nothing more.

When she returned from the kitchen, she had the bottle of whiskey tucked under one arm and two bowls in her hands—one filled with salsa, the other with tortilla chips. Buck jumped to his feet and grabbed the alcohol, so she could set the food on the table. Without a word, she spun around and headed back into the kitchen. Opening the bottle, he poured the equivalent of two shots into both glasses, then set it aside.

For the next few minutes, he heard Regina opening and closing the doors to the refrigerator and several cabinets, along with a drawer. When he asked her if she needed any help, she'd declined his offer, so he picked up his glass again and nursed the whiskey in between mouthfuls of chips and salsa. Until she'd brought them out, he'd forgotten he hadn't had dinner yet, but his stomach was growling for something a little more substantial.

Regina reappeared, this time carrying a platter with three different types of cheeses, pepperoni, soppressata, and crackers. "I had a late lunch but no dinner. I assume you haven't eaten tonight yet either. I hope this is enough —I have to go grocery shopping tomorrow. Ryan eats like food's going out of style. I forgot what it's like living with a man who can eat his own weight in steak—I'm used to sharing an apartment with two women and a full refrigerator."

He moved things out of the way, so she could place the platter on the coffee table along with two small paper plates and some napkins. "You're amazing, woman. And it's plenty—thank you."

They noshed in silence until Buck's stomach was happier than it'd been twenty minutes ago. Regina had stopped eating before he had and curled up on her end of the couch with the afghan wrapped around her again. When he leaned back against the cushions, Regina asked, "So, what about you, Buck? What are you afraid of?"

He snorted. "I'm a lean, mean, fighting machine, Gi. I ain't afraid of nuttin'."

"Ain't ain't a word. Didn't Mrs. Forsythe drill that into your and Ryan's heads back in second grade?"

A smile spread across his face. "We had her in third. Noah and Justin were in her class with us too. I think we scarred her for life and made her decide to drop a grade, to kids who were a year younger and less trouble. After that, Principal Yarro made sure the four of us were split between the two classes for fourth and fifth. If there'd been four classes per grade, I'm sure he would've put one of us in each, so we couldn't cause any more chaos."

"You all weren't that bad. At least not that I can remember."

"We weren't exactly bad—I mean, we rarely got suspended, and no one got expelled like Tommy Reed. But we did have a few teachers pulling their hair out every now and then."

"Tommy Reed? I don't remember that name. Does he still live around here?"

He shook his head. "Nope. If I remember correctly, not long after he was expelled, his folks divorced, and his mother took him and moved somewhere. I never saw him again. Hell, I'm surprised I remembered his name after all this time."

"What did he get expelled for?"

A chuckle preceded his answer. "It was when we were in fourth grade. He tossed a bunch of lit firecrackers under the principal's car, then told the guy to fuck off. He got suspended for that. The next day, he called in a bomb threat to the school. It didn't take the cops long to trace the call back to him. They expelled him, but I don't know if he got any juvie time for it. He was a weird kid—I wouldn't be surprised if his name comes up when some guy goes postal somewhere and kills a bunch of coworkers or something."

"I don't remember hearing any of that, but if you were in fourth grade, I would've been in Pre-K."

She'd been such a cute kid back then—her hair up in pigtails as she tried to follow her brother and his friends everywhere they went. Like most young boys, they'd thought their female tag-along had been a pain in the ass sometimes, but they still watched out for her.

"So, you never answered my question," Regina said after taking another sip of her whiskey. The alcohol was calming her, although the candlelight and his company were probably helping too.

"What question was that?"

"You said everyone's afraid of something, so what's *your* something?"

Reaching for the platter on the table, he snatched a piece of pepperoni and popped it into his mouth, giving himself a few moments before he had to answer. One thing he'd learned about Regina while growing up, she could be a pit bull when she wanted to know something someone wasn't telling her. She'd almost ruined the surprise party her family had thrown for her thirteenth birthday because she'd figured out something was going on. She'd hidden in Ryan's room when Buck and Noah had stopped by a few days before the party. They'd mentioned it, and a muffled squeal had come from under the bed. After dragging her out, Ryan had told her to fake being shocked at the party because their folks had been planning it for weeks. Buck had to admit, she'd been pretty damn convincing when everyone had jumped out and yelled surprise the day of the party.

A glance at her face told him she was waiting for him to answer, and she'd be pissed if he didn't. Not wanting her getting mad at him when they'd been talking like old friends again, he sighed and ran a hand down his face. He couldn't look at her as he confessed, "I'm afraid of my nightmares. I'm afraid some night I'm going to go to sleep and wake up in the middle of one of my nightmares and stay there."

There was an extended pause, and then she softly asked, "Do you suffer from PTSD?"

"Yeah."

"I'm sorry, Buck. I didn't know."

He shrugged. "I know you didn't. Most people don't. Ry and Justin do. The nightmares are the worst of it, but gunshots or cars backfiring can send me into a panic. They had to hold onto me during Mr. Scott's funeral when it was time for the twenty-one-gun salute."

Regina closed the distance between them and set a gentle hand on his shoulder. "I'm so sorry you have to go through that. It sucks that the men and women of our military can't leave what they've seen and done on the battlefield and come home without having to relive it over and over again, if only in their minds. I know Ryan has the occasional nightmares. He won't talk about them, but a few times I've heard him get up in the middle of the night. The first time, I came out to check on him because it sounded like he was stumbling around. By the time I got there, he was sitting on the floor in the kitchen with the lights off, pale and in a cold sweat. Said he just wanted to be alone and told me to go back to bed. When I hesitated, he basically ordered me to leave him alone. The next morning, he apologized and said when he gets like that, it's best to just let him work it out himself."

Buck was surprised to hear Ryan seemed to have his

own personal hell from a few tours in Afghanistan. Then again, he shouldn't be surprised. Some members of the military who'd seen combat, or the worst humanity could inflict on itself, seemed to be able to deal with it better than others—or hide it better.

"Hey, whatta you say to a game of backgammon?" Regina asked, clearly changing the subject, for which he was grateful. While she was letting him off the hook and not making him talk about an uncomfortable subject, it was also obvious she didn't want him to leave yet. Whether it was because the lights were still out or she actually wanted to spend time with him, he didn't know or really care because he didn't want to leave either. "There's enough light with the candles, and I bet I can still whip your butt."

He grinned. "You're on. And it looks like your memory is off, squirt. I was the one who kicked your butt every time."

seven

*H*er head pounding, mouth dry, and stomach roiling, Regina slowly awakened to the sunlight pouring in through the living room window. The couch was comfortable underneath her, but her head rested on something solid and unyielding. Weren't their throw pillows softer than that?

A loud snore had her eyes flying open and pushing up into a seated position. *Uuuggghhhh.* Bad move. The room spun before becoming focused again. She swallowed the urge to throw up. How much had she had to drink? From the looks of it—a lot. The bottle of whiskey that'd been unopened until last night only had about a shot or two left in it.

Beside her, Buck was asleep, sitting up. She'd been using his denim-covered thigh as a pillow. He'd stayed all night, making sure she'd felt safe during the blackout. His head was tilted back, and his feet were on the floor. His breathing was even, with the occasional snore coming from his open mouth.

Her heart squeezed. While she was grateful he'd helped comfort her and stave off a panic attack, she couldn't let that influence her. Last night, during a few spirited games of backgammon, and with the assistance of a large amount of whiskey, she'd felt the twinges of her teenage crush bubbling to the surface. Several times, her mind had gone back to the kiss they'd once shared and how good it'd been. How intoxicating. How wonderful. With the alcohol flowing through her blood stream, she'd been able to imagine a replay of that special moment over and over again, without the shitty ending. Instead, her mind had conjured up a new ending, one where she and Buck had winded up naked in bed and thoroughly sated. But now, hungover, she remembered why she'd kept her distance from him all those years—he'd hurt her and could do it again.

Taking a slow glance around the room, Regina realized the power had come back on—probably just after sunrise, since all the lights were now on and they hadn't woken her up in the middle of the night. The cable box flashed, indicating she needed to reset it so the correct time would show. Her cell was on the coffee table, amid candles that were still flickering, the whiskey bottle, two empty tumblers, and the remnants of their impromptu dinner last night. Only three crackers, five slices of cheese, some chips, and a scoop or two of salsa remained.

Leaning forward, Regina blew out the candles and grabbed her phone, bringing it to life. The device's clock read 9:23 a.m. *Hmm.*

"Shit!" She jumped up, regretting it immediately as the room rotated as if she were on a Tilt-a-Whirl.

A hand grabbed her waist, steadying her. "Easy, squirt."

Buck's voice was raspy from sleep, and she glanced down to see he didn't appear to be as hungover as she was. How his amber eyes were fully alert when he'd been passed out only a moment before was beyond her, and she didn't have time to contemplate it. Sidestepping around the coffee table, she headed for the stairs as quickly as her rebelling stomach and the thundering in her brain would allow. "I have to hurry and shower—I have to be at the sanctuary in a half hour. Shit. I hate being late."

She stopped on the fourth step and ducked down so she could see him through the spindles of the banister. "Thank you for last night. I would've been freaking out until the power came on or until the sun rose."

Buck gave her a small smile. "That's what friends are for, right?"

Friends. Right. They were nothing more than friends and had been far less than that for the past seven years. As mad and as humiliated as she'd felt about him, she really had missed his friendship. Maybe they could gain back the relationship they'd had before they'd gone and ruined it all in the blink of an eye. It took a lot of energy to hate someone and avoid them all the time, especially when they lived in the same small town. "Right . . . but, um . . . I just wanted you to know I appreciate you checking on me and staying."

"You're welcome." Pointing to the ceiling, he added, "Go shower and get ready. I'll clean up down here and let myself out."

After hesitating a moment, she nodded. "Thanks."

✿✿✿✿✿✿

"THEY'RE ADORABLE." Regina and Hogan watched an eighty-pound Bonnie play-wrestle with her hundred-pound sibling Clyde inside a large enclosure. "I've never seen bears this closeup before."

She'd sent Hogan a text as she'd been leaving her house, letting him know she was on her way. Somehow, she'd only been seven minutes late arriving at the sanctuary. As he'd promised, Buck had cleaned up the living room and kitchen before leaving her house. He'd put the old food in the garbage and the bowls and glasses in the dishwasher. Regina would run it when she got back home. He'd also left out a Gatorade, two slices of buttered toast, and a bottle of Tylenol for her. It didn't surprise her that he'd easily found things around the house—Justin, Ryan, and Buck each had keys to the others' homes and spent enough time in each to know where almost everything was. With his hangover remedies, the last of her headache and upset stomach had been slowly dissipating. Hopefully, her alcohol-induced condition wasn't evident to her new client.

"Would you like to get closer?" Hogan asked. "I've been training them since I rescued them when they were only about six weeks old. Since I knew they weren't going to be able to be released back into the wild, I've been imprinting myself on them—I play and interact with them for hours, every day, and they know I make the rules. I'll have them lie down and Clyde will let you pet him if I tell him to."

Her eyes widened. "Seriously?"

"Yup. I've actually been approached by a casting director for some movie they want Clyde to be in. We're still in negotiations because I want to be certain he'll be safe during the filming."

"Wow. Um, yeah, I'd love to get closer, if you think it's okay."

He smiled and gestured to a door in the heavy fence. "Come on. He loves belly rubs."

A few minutes later, Regina's heart was pounding in her chest as she knelt next to the male black bear, rubbing the thick, coarse fur covering his belly. She was in total awe of being close enough to a wild animal to touch it and not have it want to eat her. Clyde's powerful paws and claws were huge and foretold how much bigger the bear would grow when he reached full adulthood. After feeding them some blueberries, with a promise of more to come if they were good, Hogan had gotten both bears to lay on their backs, side by side, while he squatted between their heads.

"This is incredible. I've only seen bears from a distance and was always told to give them a wide berth."

"Any other bear, I'd say that's definitely the best thing to do. But these two have been living with me since I rescued them." He jutted his chin toward the one-floor ranch he called home on the other side of the dirt driveway she'd parked on. "Talk about a handful. They got into everything. When they started flipping over the kitchen table just for fun, I knew it was time to move them out here. They sleep in the shelter over there at night and play out here during the day when I can't be with them. I spend at least ten hours a day with them,

SAMANTHA A. COLE

making sure they come to rely on me for everything. When the weather was warmer, I'd swim with them in a pool we just took down a few weeks ago. We set up a fence around the new enclosure, so they can hang out with me while I'm in there working with the two guys helping me build it. If the bears were older than they are now, I wouldn't trust them with people who had to turn their backs on them, but for now, they're still too young and small to do any damage aside from the occasional nip when they think they're being ignored."

Regina glanced around. "This place is amazing. You said you'd gotten donations from people to get it up and running, right?"

"Yeah. Some of it was my savings, but that was never going to last for long, so I started making phone calls and connections. I did a video interview a few months ago for the local paper, and it went viral after they posted it on their website. They'd suggested I start an online fundraiser before the story went live because animal lovers would probably want to donate whatever they could, and they were right. We raised over thirty-thousand dollars in under a week just through that campaign. But then I was contacted by a few philanthropists, including Largo Ridge's own Sadie Kemp, who donated much larger sums."

"Mrs. Kemp is my friend Zia's grandmother. She loves a good cause."

He chuckled. "That she does. But she'd only make the donation if I agreed to let her meet Bonnie and Clyde and take a picture with them. That'd been a no-brainer. The bears were a bit smaller then, and she was thrilled about the photo op. She's a sweet lady and stops in to check on things once every few weeks, making sure we have everything we need for the animals."

"How many more animals do you have?"

"Bonnie and Clyde are the only two permanent ones staying with us at the moment, but there's a peregrine falcon and a fox currently going through rehabilitation for injuries and three fawns and two raccoons that are orphans. All of them will be released back into the wild when we're certain they can survive."

Clyde suddenly sneezed, his big body jerking, and Regina yelped and yanked her hands away from his belly before realizing she wasn't in any danger. Laughing, she reached out and gave him a few more scratches. "Well, as much as I'd love to stay out here and play with you two all day, I think your daddy and I have some business to attend to."

"Yes, we do." He stood and held out a hand. When she took it, he helped her to her feet. Clyde and Bonnie both rolled over and got up on all four paws. Sticking their faces into the two buckets filled with blueberries, they began to scarf them down.

Regina watched in amazement for a moment, then let Hogan lead her out of the enclosure, across the yard, and into his house.

eight

*I*n the middle of spackling the drywall in the dining room, Buck was surprised to get a text from Regina.

Gi: Thanks again for last night and also for cleaning up and leaving the hangover stuff out.

Buck: No problem. How was your meeting with Hogan?

Gi: It was good. Thanks for hooking me up with him too.

He sent her a thumbs-up emoji followed by an upside-down smiley face. There was a long pause, and he figured she was done with the chat, but just as he was about to set the cell phone back down on a stool next to a bottle of water, it chimed again.

Gi: Are you doing anything for dinner tonight?

He was taken aback but was all for having dinner with her.

Buck: What did you have in mind?

Gi: Red Door?

The Red Door Saloon was a pub popular with the locals as well as tourists. They had excellent food, and if you were from Largo Ridge, it was a sure bet you'd run into at least a few people you knew there on any given night. Whenever Buck had come home to visit between deployments, he'd always made sure he stopped into the saloon at least once or twice.

Buck: Sounds good. Six okay?

Gi: Yup. I'll meet you there.

Buck: See you then.

Setting his phone down, he picked up the bottle of water and took a long drink. Dinner, sort of, with Regina two nights in a row? Yeah, that was pretty shocking. Last night, as soon as the transformer had blown, knocking out the power in the area, he'd worried about her, knowing how much she hated the dark. Not that he blamed her after the scare she'd had when she'd been a young kid. He'd raced over to the Vaughns' place, and it was a good thing he had. She'd been on the verge of a complete meltdown, despite the candles she'd lit. After they'd broken out the marble backgammon set her father had taught them all to play on, she'd relaxed even more— although the shots of whiskey probably had more to do with that than Buck being there.

He had to admit, it'd felt great hanging out with her again. They'd razzed each other during the multiple backgammon games they'd played, laughed, and just talked about stuff. Wisely, Buck had avoided subjects such as if she was dating again and why she'd called off her wedding at the last minute. Ryan had told him the latter had been because she'd realized she wasn't in love with her fiancé, and Buck wondered why she'd agreed to marry the guy in the first place if that'd been the case. But the last thing he'd wanted to do during the hours they'd played and talked was hear about the man she'd almost married or that she was dating anyone now that she was "on the market" again, as a guy he knew would say. Buck actually hated that phrase—it made a woman sound like a side of beef.

While Buck wasn't going to do anything stupid with Regina, like kiss her again, he did want to get their friendship back on an even keel. He'd missed her. The problem with that was he really did want to kiss her again. If she'd made a pass at him last night, it would've been hard to refuse her. She'd been beautiful at nineteen, but at twenty-six, she was fucking gorgeous. Her curves had filled out, and her face had matured more. The woman was a knockout and it grated on him thinking of her dating any of the jackasses in Largo

Ridge who were just looking to put another notch on their bedposts.

Glancing at his watch, he got back to work. He had about four hours before he would need to hop into the shower in order to meet Regina on time. With Ryan out of town and Justin covering the resort for the weekend, Buck was on his own today. They'd split the resort into sections, with each of them being in charge of specific areas—Ryan had kept his position as head of maintenance, with his staff fixing whatever needed to be fixed or updated throughout the entire resort. Justin maintained the ski slopes and their lifts, the sledding hills, and the snowboarding half-pipe. While they didn't have any black diamond hills for expert skiers, they did have beginner and intermediate slopes. There was a larger ski resort about twenty minutes away in the town of Bellewood, and LRSR had a shuttle bus to transport skiers who wanted the more challenging slopes back and forth. For those learning how to ski, LRSR also had two ski instructors on staff.

In addition to being in charge of the outdoor ice-skating rink, Buck had taken over running the main hotel, along with Grace, which included both indoor and outdoor pools. There were several hot tubs on the rear patio, a game room that had tables for billiards, foosball, ping-pong, and poker, and a bookcase full of board games. A bar and restaurant were also available, as well as a small spa.

The resort was a lot of work, but they had an excellent staff in place. With over fifty full-time employees and thirty part-timers, the place ran like a well-oiled machine.

Next to the main hotel was a small cottage that housed their first-aid station manned from 8:00 a.m. to 11:00 p.m. by two EMTs and backed up by local EMS during the ski season.

In the winter, when the mountains were full of snow, which was usually from mid-November to the middle of April, depending on the temperatures, was when LRSR was the busiest. From what Grace had told them, they made three quarters of their revenue during that time. While they were normally completely booked on the weekends, they had a majority of the rooms filled during the week too. When the warmer weather rolled around during the spring, they'd switch over to summer activities, of which there were plenty to attract visitors.

Not for the first time, Buck sent up a prayer of thanks to Matthew for entrusting his resort to them. It couldn't have come at a better time for him, and his best friends had been just as grateful. While she wasn't there often, Maxi helped out when she could. The men completely understood that her veterinarian practice took precedence and were okay with her being a relatively silent partner.

As he moved to tape and spackle the next seam between the drywall sheets, his phone rang. Glancing down at it, he saw it was his mother calling. She'd moved to North Carolina to be near his sister, who was eight years his senior.

Becky was an orthopedist, married to her high school sweetheart, Aaron Williams, and the mother of two adorable little girls, Mia and Hannah. Buck got down there as often as he could to visit with them, but now with the resort, he probably wouldn't get to see them again until at least March.

He picked up the phone and connected the call. "Hey, Mom."

"Hi, honey. Just calling to check on you. I haven't talked to you all week."

He smiled and leaned against the wall. "Yeah, we've been pretty busy getting ready for the snow season. How are you doing?"

He spent the next ten minutes talking his mother out of fixing him up with her friend's niece, who'd just moved to Largo Ridge. Lately, Buck hadn't had time to date, and even if he had, he'd be hard pressed to find a woman he was attracted to as much as he was to Regina.

Damn it.

nine

"You're an idiot, Regina. An absolute idiot. And you're also going insane because you're talking out loud to yourself, calling yourself an idiot." She had no idea what had made her ask Buck to dinner, but it was too late to take it back now—it was five after six, she was standing in the parking lot of the Red Door Saloon, and Buck's pickup truck was parked a few spots down from her SUV.

"This is not a date. It's two old friends having dinner together and catching up. Nothing more." *So why did you spend an hour and a half trying to decide what to wear, blowing out your hair, and putting on more than just your usual eyeliner? And seriously, you're wearing heels instead of boots or sneakers. Nope, you're not interested in having him notice you as a woman. Two old friends? Get real, Gi.*

She really hated when her inner goddess went all sarcastic. Although, with the temperatures dropping drastically from earlier in the day, she really was regretting putting on her black, open-toe pumps instead of something warmer. Under her black wool peacoat, she was wearing a rust-colored sweater with three-quarter length sleeves and a deep V-neck. A lacy, ivory camisole hid some of the way-too-suggestive cleavage the sweater exposed. The hem of the knitted top landed just below her hips. Black jeggings completed the outfit.

Are you just going to stand out here freezing your ass off or what?

Sighing, she told the little voice in her head to fuck off and walked toward the front door of the pub. The parking lot was almost full, which wasn't unusual for the Saturday night dinner crowd, however, a band would be playing tonight, starting at 9:00 p.m. By that point there would be no spaces left in the lot, leaving the latecomers to park up and down Myrtle Avenue and its side streets.

As she reached the front door, Regina took a moment to read the flyer taped to it. To her delight, it announced that Second Avenue, a local band, was playing tonight. It'd been a few years since she'd last heard them. They covered mostly classic rock from the seventies and eighties, with the occasional song from earlier or later decades thrown in. The lead guitarist and drummer were both silver foxes and had a throng of female admirers showing up wherever they played. At least the music would be good if she was still there after dinner and, hopefully, not making a fool of herself.

Damn it. Why did Buck have to be so good-looking? She'd already planned to have a drink or two because it would be easier to relax around him with the help of alcohol.

She'd realized during the day that, while his rejection

years ago still stung, she didn't hate him anymore. She'd missed him more than she thought she had. Last night had been fun—despite the blackout and her near panic attack. It'd felt like old times again, when she'd hung out with her brother's friends, talking and laughing, whether he was around or not. She'd always felt comfortable with Noah, Justin, and Buck, having known them all her life. At least she had until she'd returned home for the summer after her first year in college. That's when she'd developed a crush on Buck. She'd noticed him as a man for the first time and had visualized many fantasies with him starring in each one. Then he'd kissed her, and the resulting humiliation wasn't anything she'd expected. A few months later, she'd been so grief-stricken over her parents' deaths, she'd allowed him to console her, as all her and Ryan's other friends and family members had done, but had still kept him at arm's length. After that, she'd avoided him as much as she could.

All right, Gi. Pull up your big-girl panties and get over it. You two have a chance to be friends again. The past is the past—leave it there.

When a couple walked up behind her, she knew she could stall no longer. Pulling open the door, she strode inside. There was a loud din from a combination of conversations and the latest Zac Brown Band song playing on the jukebox. She stepped aside to let the couple move past her as she scanned the bodies and faces of the patrons gathered around the bar and sitting in the dining area. During the first pass, she didn't see Buck but was certain he was in there somewhere because his truck was outside. When she glanced around again, she slowed and double-checked each group with men in it. Her gaze flew by a woman with long blonde hair, with her back to Regina, but then the woman shifted to the side and sitting on a stool in front of her was Buck.

For a brief moment, Regina's mouth watered. He was wearing a snug, black, long-sleeved T-shirt, jeans, and Timberland boots. He'd shaved before he'd come out because there wasn't so much as a hint of a five-o'clock shadow, which he usually had by the end of the day. Her heart fluttered under her ribs, but then she stilled, and her mouth went dry. The blonde had moved closer to Buck and was running a seductive finger up and down his arm. Jealousy roared through Regina.

No, no, no! You're not supposed to be jealous, Gi. Buck can date and flirt with anyone he wants to, and you're supposed to ignore it.

Her inner goddess really needed to shut the fuck up right now because there was no way Regina was going to be a third wheel around that floozy tonight. She was about to turn around when the saloon's owner spotted her from his post behind the bar. "Regina Vaughn! Get your butt over here and give me a hug, woman!"

Her face flushed when most of the patrons at the bar turned to look at her. Robert "Red" O'Neill was an Irishman, through and through. He was about sixty-five years old and knew every local who'd come into his bar more than once. Standing five foot eight, the red-haired, green-eyed man was robust in both stature and personality. Regina didn't think there was a single person who'd ever met the man who didn't like him immediately. She'd been so busy the last several months, between

69

moving, getting settled in, and starting her new job, among other things, that she'd only been to the saloon twice since returning to Largo Ridge. Both times Red hadn't been there for one reason or another. She'd kept telling herself she had to stop in when he was there some day or night just to say hello. He'd been good friends with her parents and had held and paid for the luncheon following their funeral, refusing to take a penny from Ryan or Regina to cover the cost.

Well, so much for sneaking back out the door before Buck spotted her. She could feel his intense gaze on her as she pasted on a smile and stepped over to the bar. Red came out from behind it, leaving two other bartenders to wait on the patrons, and enveloped her in his arms, hugging her tightly for a moment before letting her go. He grasped her upper arms and nudged her back a step before looking her up and down. "You're looking more and more like your mother every time I see you."

She rolled her eyes and smirked. "Just what every woman wants to hear." Setting her hand on his chest, she patted him affectionately. "How are you, Red?"

"Well, if you came in more often, young lady, you'd already have the answer to that, now wouldn't you?"

"You are correct, and I do apologize. I've been here a few times since I moved back, but you weren't, so that has to count for something, right?"

He scowled at her for a moment, then burst out laughing. "You always could talk your way out of trouble." After glancing over his shoulder and the ever-increasing crowd, he asked, "So, who are you meeting? I'll point you in their direction if they're here already."

"That would be me, Red. Thanks." Buck's deep voice sent a shiver down Regina's spine, and she looked up at him. She hadn't seen him approach, but with the number of people in the bar, that wasn't surprising. A peek down the bar told her the blonde was still standing next to the seat he'd vacated and was glaring at Regina. Now that she could see the woman's face, she recognized her. Margo Shaw had been a year ahead of Regina in school and the head cheerleader in Regina's junior year. Wonderful. Not only did Regina have to compete with a stuck-up woman, she had to compete with a cheerleader and homecoming queen to boot.

Wait a minute! Who said Margo, or any other woman for that matter, was competition? God, she wished she could get her mind, body, and heart all on the same level when it came to Buck. He was going to date other women, and probably marry one someday, whether Regina liked it or not. Well, at least she could attempt to thwart the ones who weren't good enough away from him.

Going up on her toes, she set her hands on his shoulders for balance and kissed his cheek. The surprised look on his face was almost comical. Before either of them could say anything, Red patted her on the back. "Go take a seat. What can I get you?"

"Mic Ultra," she responded. "Thanks, Red."

As the man returned to his post where several customers were waiting for another round, Buck gestured for Regina to walk in front of him toward the stool that had his jacket hanging on the back. By the time they got there, Red had already set a cold beer bottle next to Buck's glass of Guinness. From behind, Buck helped her out of her wool peacoat and draped it over his own. There were no other available stools, so he turned it slightly toward her. "Have a seat. Red, put Gi's beer on my tab."

Margo's glare hardened. Apparently, the usually gentlemanly Buck hadn't offered his seat to her earlier. He gestured between the two women. "Margo, I don't know if you remember Ryan's sister, Regina. Gi, this is Margo—"

"Shaw," she finished for him. Regina might have a problem saying no to a lot of people, but she had no trouble standing up to bullies and bitches. Margo Shaw was definitely the latter. Pretending to be polite, Regina smiled and held out her hand. "I was a year behind you in school. How are you?"

As expected, Margo's handshake was on the limp side —typical of a woman who didn't want to be shaking hands with someone she perceived as a rival. "Fine. I'm sorry, but I don't remember you."

Regina shrugged. "No biggie. The only reason I recognized you was because I remembered you face-planted stepping off the homecoming float after the parade my junior year."

Margo's eyes widened, and her face reddened with rage. Beside Regina, she barely heard Buck stifle an amused snort.

"That was you, wasn't it?" Regina's words dripped with saccharin, as she crossed her legs.

The other woman looked like she was about to explode. She glowered at Regina for a few moments, then straightened her spine. Without another word to her new nemesis, she pasted on a fake smile, as Regina had done several minutes earlier, and turned to Buck. "If you'll excuse me, I'll talk to you some other time." She gave Regina another evil eye glare before her gaze met Buck's again. "That is, whenever you want better company than her. It shouldn't be too long."

Clearly, Margo wasn't quick with witty comebacks because that one had been lame. After she stormed off, Buck burst out laughing, but low enough that Margo couldn't hear him. "Holy shit, woman. That was awesome, and I remember that! Someone sent me a video of it when I was overseas. My entire platoon watched it. Anyway, I've been trying to get rid of her for the past fifteen minutes, so thank you for finally showing up."

Regina's eyebrows shot up. She'd assumed Buck had been interested in Margo. At her expression, he shook his head. "Nope, not my type. She's been hitting on me for years. Justin banged her a couple of times about ten years ago, and ever since then she's been trying to nail me and Ryan. She hit on Noah too, but we all had an agreement."

"Bros before hos, right?" she asked. Yeah, she'd heard Ryan and his friends say that a few times when they'd been younger.

Buck, at least, had the decency to look chagrined. "Something like that. We also didn't hit on anyone's ex-girlfriend."

Before Regina could respond, another woman—an attractive brunette in her mid to late twenties—walked up and tapped Buck on the shoulder. "Buck, your table is ready when you are."

He smiled at her. "Thanks, Melissa. Oh, hey, have you two met yet?" When both women shook their heads, Buck took care of the introductions. "Gi, this is Red's cousin's daughter. She and her mom and two-year-old daughter moved to Largo Ridge a few months ago, and Melissa started working here as the hostess on Fridays and Saturdays." His gaze shifted to the younger woman. "This is Ryan Vaughn's sister, Regina."

Relieved this wasn't another woman coming to hit on Buck while she was there, Regina held out her hand to Melissa. "It's nice to meet you."

The hostess grinned and shook her hand and not in the wishy-washy way Margo had. "Hi, it's nice to meet you too. Ryan talks about you all the time."

"He does?"

"Yup, he does. He's very proud of you."

Surprised, Regina glanced back and forth between Melissa and Buck, who nodded in agreement. Ryan often told her he was proud of her, but she never knew he was in the habit of telling other people that too. "Wow. Um . . . thank you."

"Don't thank me, thank him," she said with a laugh. "Anyway, your table is ready. It's the one in the far corner, next to the front window. I already put menus down for you."

"Thanks." Buck picked up both their drinks. "Grab our coats, Gi. I don't know about you, but I'm starving."

ten

On their way through the crowd and then around the occupied tables, they said quick hellos to quite a few people they knew. When they reached their assigned table, which was large enough for four people but set for two, Regina hung their coats on the back of a chair, then sat on the one next to it. Buck placed their drinks down on the table and took the seat across from her. Ever since he'd spotted her walking into the place, he'd been having a hard time trying not to drool over her. Margo Shaw had nothing on Regina Vaughn.

Usually, she had her hair up in a ponytail, but tonight, she'd blown it out into soft waves that framed her pretty face. Subtle makeup enhanced her facial features, while delicate gold jewelry adorned her ears and neck. A dropped charm necklace drew his gaze down to the V of her sweater. Ivory lace covered a portion of her cleavage, but it was still sexy as hell. What he wouldn't give to have the right to reach over and run his finger along the top of the lace. While the sweater covered her hips, it fit snugly and didn't do much to hide her curves. Having friends and acquaintances calling out greetings to him on the way to the table had made him lift his gaze and helped prevent him from tripping over other people's feet because he'd been focused on her ass.

Setting his menu aside—he'd already checked out the sign that announced tonight's dinner specials—he folded his arms on the table. "So, what prompted you to ask me out to dinner?"

Her jaw dropped, and her cheeks pinkened. "I-I . . . um, I didn't *ask* you out to dinner, I asked if you wanted to have dinner with me."

Damn, she was adorable when she was flustered. But now she had him confused. "Isn't that the same thing?"

"No." That one word came out short and crisp, as if the entire conversation should be obvious, but it wasn't.

Buck frowned. "What do you mean, 'no'?"

"Asking you to dinner sounds like a date, which is not what this is."

A chuckle erupted from his chest. "It isn't? Then what is it?" He couldn't help but tease her.

Her explanation came out slowly, as if she were talking to a child. "This is two *friends* having dinner together. Nothing more."

"Are you sure?"

"Buck!"

The exasperation in her tone had him laughing louder this time. "All right, I'm just teasing you. You're too easy, Gi."

When her tense shoulders relaxed, he changed the subject. As much fun as it was to razz her, insinuating this was a date would probably cause trouble. The last thing he wanted was for her to get mad at him and start avoiding him again. "So, I spoke to Hogan a little while ago. He was impressed with you. He also told me you got up close and personal with Bonnie and Clyde. Aren't they awesome?"

Her eyes lit up. "Oh my God, they're amazing! I can't believe I was petting a live bear. I'll never be able to hear about someone hunting bears without thinking of the two of them now. It's going to piss me off."

While Buck and his friends had never gone hunting for bear, which was legal during certain seasons in New Hampshire, they had hunted deer in their teens. But after being in combat in the military, killing the enemy and seeing soldiers he'd served with die, he'd sworn he would never hunt another living thing unless his life or an innocent person's life depended on it.

Their waitress came over, and after they ordered another round of drinks, Regina announced she knew what she wanted for dinner if he was ready too. Once the waitress left them alone, Buck steered the conversation toward everyday things. They had a good time talking about different subjects. In fact, Buck couldn't remember the last time he'd enjoyed a date that much—not that it was a date, at least, according to Regina. What he liked most about talking with her was that most of her statements didn't start with an "I," like Margo's had earlier, or the last few women he'd hooked up with. Regina gave her opinion but was also interested in his. He was enjoying her company so much he barely remembered being served their dinner and eating it. That was the Regina he'd known and loved like family growing up, but now, she was much more than that. This Regina was the one he could find himself falling for, and honestly, that scared the shit out of him. The last thing he wanted to do was hurt her, and with his PTSD, there was always a chance that could happen.

When their check arrived, Buck snatched it before Regina could. She glared at him when he wouldn't let her see it. "This isn't a date, Buck. We're splitting that."

"Nope. Call it whatever you want, but I've got it this time. You can leave the tip."

That seemed to placate her a little. "Fine, but can I see the total, so I know how much to leave?"

Since it was a reasonable request, he relented. Their waitress returned and took the check back along with the credit card he'd pulled out of his wallet. Across the pub, on a small stage, the band was getting set up. As much as he wanted to stay and hang out with Regina and listen to the music, he had to get up early in the morning. They were coming down to the wire, getting the resort ready for the ski season, so they'd all been putting in six-day weeks. Tomorrow, he was doing a walkthrough of all the public areas and any empty guest rooms with the assistant manager, Theodora Fisher, who worked every other weekend, to make certain nothing was in need of any last-minute repairs. They'd make note of what needed to be fixed and give to Ryan on Monday.

During the week, in addition to preparing for the ski season, they also had to start planning for Halloween. Every year, LRSR ran haunted hayrides for a full week leading up to the holiday. Then the night before

Halloween, they would host a scavenger hunt, a pumpkin carving contest, and a costume party for their guests and local townspeople. It was one of Buck's favorite times at the resort. As a kid, he'd gone to all the events as a guest, but when they'd gotten older, Noah, Ryan, Justin, and he had joined the resort's staff and some local teens working the events. The best had been the haunted hayride. Dressing up like Jason, Freddy Kruger, and other scary characters or monsters, they'd taken great delight in jumping out from behind trees and scaring the crap out of people.

"I'd really like to stay and listen to the band, but honestly, I'm beat," Regina said as she stuck a generous tip under the saltshaker. "Would you mind if I cut out?"

She did look tired, but he wasn't going to tell her that. "I'm not surprised, since we only had about five hours of sleep last night. And no, I don't mind. In fact, I've got to be at the resort early tomorrow, so I'm going to walk out with you."

Once the waitress returned his credit card, Buck stood and helped Regina into her coat before pulling on his own. It took them a good ten or fifteen minutes to get out of there, since several people stopped one or the other, or both, to talk on their way to the door. Red came from around the bar to give Regina another hug and to shake hands with Buck. When they finally exited to the parking lot, a cold breeze wrapped around them. The temperature had dropped from around fifty-eight degrees during the day, to just above freezing, hours after the sun had set.

Regina tugged her peacoat tighter around her torso, and Buck glanced down at her feet. Her shoes were sexy and added about three inches to her height, but they weren't ideal for cold weather. She wasn't a southern transplant who didn't know any better, so had she worn them for him? Heat pooled in his groin and caused his dick to twitch at the thought, despite the cold weather.

Like the gentleman his parents had raised, he escorted Regina to her vehicle. She used a key fob to unlock the SUV, and he opened the driver's door for her. Before she climbed in, she turned to face him. "Thank you, again, for last night. You helped me avoid a total panic attack."

"It was my pleasure," he said truthfully as he gazed into her dark-blue eyes. Hell, he could stare at her all day and night and never get tired of it.

The wind lifted her beautiful, black hair, scattering a few strands, and he reached over and tucked them behind her ear. "It was also nice to catch up with you. I've missed you, Gi." Her eyes widened at his unexpected confession, and she licked her lips, drawing his attention to them. They were plump and pink and looked so damn kissable.

Aw, hell. He couldn't help himself. Lowering his head, he kept his gaze on her delectable mouth. He was barely an inch away from kissing her, when she shoved against his chest, backing him up a few steps. Fire flared in her eyes, and her face hardened. "No. You don't get to do that again, Buck. You didn't like it last time, remember? You apologized and ran without an explanation. Was I that bad of a kisser?" His mouth dropped, and she held up a hand. "You know what? Don't answer that because I really don't want to know if that was the reason."

"What the hell? How could you think . . ." Before he

could finish his question, she spun around and started to climb into the driver's seat. *Oh, hell no.*

Grasping her upper arm, he pulled until she crashed into his own body. Taking her other arm, he helped her get her balance before he stepped forward and pinned her against the rear passenger door. She gaped at him as he got into her face. "Is that what you think? That I left because you were a bad kisser? Seriously, Gi?"

Not waiting for an answer, he cupped her jaw and crushed his mouth down on hers. He melded their lips together and took advantage of her open mouth, sweeping his tongue inside to duel with hers. She was rigid at first, but then she melted. Her arms went around his neck, and her fingers brushed against the hair just above his nape.

Bad kisser? Hell no. She was a freaking amazing kisser, at least she was with him. Christ, it was even better than he remembered. Regina gave as much as he offered. He cursed the fact they were standing in a parking lot and not someplace where he could strip her naked and worship her body the way it deserved to be.

A car pulled into the lot, casting its headlights over them for a brief moment. Buck slowed the kiss until he finally lifted his head just far enough to look into her eyes, which were filled with shock, passion, and need. "Me walking out like an ass, without an explanation, had nothing to do with how you kissed me, Gi, and everything to do with the fact you were nineteen and naive, with your whole life ahead of you. I was twenty-six and trying to come to terms with the things I'd done and seen in the Middle East. I was already damaged and couldn't let that damage touch you. You were a bright light, and the last thing I wanted to do was to extinguish that light with the darkness inside me. I'm sorry I hurt you."

Her gaze dropped to his chest. "You didn't hurt me," she mumbled.

"Liar."

Her chin lifted, and anger filled her face for the second time tonight. She pushed against his chest, this time forcing him back a step. Damn it, he'd fucked up—again.

"Go to hell, Buck." She climbed into her vehicle, and this time he let her. Without another word, she closed the door, started the engine, and raced out of the parking lot. As he watched the taillights disappear around a bend in the road, his gut clenched. Like an idiot, he'd hurt her once more, but this time, he wasn't going to wait seven years to make it up to her and, ultimately, kiss her again. Because . . . shit . . . because he was still fucking in love with her after all that time.

eleven

"Hey, what are you doing here?" Buck asked Justin as he strolled into the garage attached to the maintenance building where Ryan's office was. Justin had the hood of his Chevy Silverado up and was bent over the engine, tinkering with it.

"Giving the truck a tune-up. Changing the filters and oil and stuff. Not going to have much time to do it in another week or so."

"Yeah, I was planning on doing mine one night this week too."

He leaned against the front quarter panel and watched his friend work for a few minutes. Justin lifted a brow at him. "What's on your mind?"

"What makes you think anything is?"

"Because, dude, you're standing there, not saying a word, and watching me change a fan belt like it's the most interesting thing in the world. Now, fess up. What's going on?"

He shrugged. "I need some advice."

Standing erect, Justin pulled a rag out of the back pocket of his jeans and wiped his hands. "Shoot."

Buck hesitated a moment, trying to figure out how to explain his dilemma without giving his friend too much information. "There's this girl . . . woman, who I've known for a while, and I really like her. Like she's all I can think about now, and I'm scared to start anything with her."

"Why's that?"

"This PTSD crap. I'm afraid I'm going to have a flashback when I'm with her and freak out. I mean, shit, what if I wake up from a nightmare swinging and I hurt her?"

Justin eyed him. "When was the last time you slept with a woman? I mean, actually slept with one?"

His gaze dropped to the floor, and he shuffled his feet in embarrassment. "It's been a while. A long while. I don't want to hurt anyone."

"I can understand that. I've woken a few times, not sure where I was and who I was with." He crossed his arms and leaned his hip against the front of the truck. "Does this chick know you have PTSD?"

"It came up in a conversation, but she doesn't know the full extent of it. And she's not a chick."

The corners of his mouth raised. "Sorry. Okay, so this *woman* knows about your PTSD. Was she sympathetic and understanding or did she blow it off like it was probably just all in your head and it wasn't real?"

Buck thought back to the talk he'd had with Regina the night the power had gone out. "No, she definitely got it. Didn't blow it off at all."

"That's a plus. Listen, Buck, you can't spend your life alone. If you care for this woman and want something more than a one- or two-night stand with her, then you're going to have to take a step forward and see if she can handle your PTSD. If she's the one for you, she'll stand by you through thick or thin—flashbacks, nightmares, and all. And if she's not, you'll know it soon enough. The one thing I learned about losing Noah the way we did was to make sure when it's your time to go, don't have any regrets about chances you never took."

Sticking his hands into the front pockets of his jeans, Buck asked, "Do you think he had regrets?"

Justin lifted a shoulder. "I don't know. I'd like to think he didn't, but only he and our maker know the answer to that. I just hope I don't have any down the line, and I hope you and Ryan don't either."

Inhaling deeply, he let out the breath slowly. There were a lot of things in his adult life he regretted—among them, not being able to say goodbye to his father when the old man had suffered a massive heart attack and passed away, the blood on his hands from combat, and running out on Regina all those years ago. "I already have a bunch of regrets—some I can't do anything about—but maybe I can turn at least one of them around."

"So, you're gonna ask her out?"

A smile spread across his face. "Yeah, I think I will."

"Good." Justin stuck his head under the hood again and began unscrewing the top to the air filter housing. "Hand me that new filter over there."

Glancing around, Buck saw a box sitting on top of a large, red toolbox and stepped over to grab it. He opened it and handed the filter to Justin. "Thanks. So, when are you going to tell Ryan that you want to date his sister?"

Taken aback, he froze as his eyes grew to the size of saucers. "Shit, how did you know it was Gi I was talking about?"

His friend smirked. "I didn't know for certain until just now. I suspected you had a thing for her years ago, but then something changed between you two, sometime around the Vaughns' funeral. What happened?"

Leave it to one of his best buddies to see right through him. He ran a frustrated hand through his hair. "I kissed her, but it was before Mr. & Mrs. V. were killed. It just happened, and I freaked out afterward for a few reasons. I apologized and took off, not realizing I'd hurt her by not staying and explaining how I felt and why it would be better if I let her find someone who didn't have blood on his hands. She's barely said a word to me over the past seven years, with the exception of at the Vaughns' and Noah's funerals." A thought occurred to him. "Shit, do you think Ry knows I kissed her and then ran?"

"Did he kick your ass over it?"

Relieved, Buck snorted. "You're right—he doesn't know."

"Yeah, well, you better tell him before you take things to the next level. And don't expect him not to try to kick your ass just for thinking of Gi like that."

The guy was right again. And it looked like he was going to have to throw down with his best friend, because Buck had every intention of taking things to the next level with Regina, whether she realized it yet or not.

Sɪɢʜɪɴɢ, Regina threw a few files she wanted to work on that evening into her briefcase before grabbing her purse. It'd been a long day, and she was still brewing over how things had ended between her and Buck the other night. What annoyed her most was she was reliving that kiss they'd shared more than what had happened in the moments after it. She'd almost accepted his apology and explanation of why he'd walked away from her seven years ago, but then he'd branded her a liar about not being hurt. The truth was, she had been lying—she'd just gotten pissed he'd called her on it. And now she looked like a petulant child who'd had a tantrum in front of him. Crap.

"Night, Regina," the receptionist, Megan O'Brien, said as Regina walked past her desk. It was just after five, and the other woman was shutting down her computer for the evening.

"Night, Megan. See you tomorrow."

Pushing open the door, she stepped into the hallway that led to the lobby of the building Carney & Brewer shared with five other business offices. From there, she would take the stairs down one flight to the employees-only parking garage. Regina was sure in a few weeks she'd be grateful for four cement walls that kept out most of the elements. Her car would warm up much faster in there than if she'd parked in the outside lot.

A few people from the other offices were also on their way out and she exchanged short, friendly greetings with a few of them. Reaching the garage level, she turned left toward where she'd parked her SUV that morning. As she approached, she was dismayed to see the front tire of the vehicle was flat. "Well, shit."

Thankfully, her father had demanded she learn how to change a tire before allowing her to get her driver's license. It just really sucked she'd have to do it while wearing a pair of dress pants, her favorite sweater, and pumps.

Walking between her SUV and the car next to it, she stopped short when she saw the rear tire was in the same condition as the front one. "What the hell?"

Her brow furrowing, she hurried around to the passenger side, only to find both those tires were flat as well. Glancing around, she didn't see anyone watching her. A car driven by one of the women she'd descended the stairs behind was pulling up to the yellow arm of the security gate. While it kept unauthorized people from driving in, it didn't stop anyone from walking in.

Digging into the outside pocket of her purse, she found her cell phone and hit the speed dial for Ryan. Nothing happened. Shit. The walls of the garage were interfering with her service. Unlocking the SUV, she put her bag and briefcase on the passenger seat, then locked the door again. She moved closer to the exit and when she finally saw a few more bars pop up, she tried to place the call again. This time it went through.

"Hey, Gi, what's up?"

Through a combination of anger and a few frustrated tears, she told her brother what'd happened.

"Shit, Gi. Is anyone around?"

She checked her surroundings again. "Just a few people leaving for the day."

"I'm on my way. I want you to go back up to your office and call the police."

"The police? Why?" Even as she asked it, she knew it was a stupid question. "Never mind. No one has four flat tires unless someone did it purposely. I'll call the police after I hang up with you."

"No, I want you to go back to your office until I get there—or the police do. Call from there. It's safer."

"All right, I'm going."

Disconnecting the call, she strode quickly back to her car, retrieved her purse and briefcase, and decided to take the elevator back up the one flight. She suddenly had no urge to be in the stairwell by herself. She watched the only three people in the elevator get out and walk away before she stepped into it.

The front door to the CPA office was still unlocked, which meant there were still people inside, which wasn't uncommon. A quick glance around revealed two of her coworkers were still at their desks, Mr. Carney was in his office, talking on the phone, and one of the other senior CPAs was at his desk with an open file, punching the buttons on his calculator. None of them paid her any attention.

Taking a seat at her desk, she called the non-emergency line for the Largo Ridge Police Department. It was one of those phone numbers she knew by heart from her elementary school days when she'd gone through the D.A.R.E. program with her classmates. After relaying the nature of her call, she was told an officer would be responding shortly and she should wait in her office until he arrived.

Ten minutes later, she was back down in the parking garage with Officer Luke Atwater. He was kind of cute and around her age. If he'd gone to school in Largo Ridge, he hadn't been in Regina's class. While he was taking down her information and asking if she knew of any reason why someone would slash her tires—yes, he'd discovered someone had sliced them with a knife—he was also flirting with her. She was flattered but not to the point she flirted back.

The patrolman was taking photos of her vehicle when Ryan and Buck strode past the downed arm of the gate and headed for her. Buck reached her first, his concerned gaze raking over her. "Gi, what the hell happened?"

Not wanting to let her brother in on the fact she and Buck were having personal issues, Regina acted as normal as one could be after finding someone had slashed her tires. "I don't know. I came down to leave for the night and found all four tires flat. Officer Atwater said someone sliced them with a knife."

"Fuck," Ryan murmured as he circled around the vehicle and introduced himself to the cop.

Buck glanced up and slowly turned a full circle on the ball of his foot. "There're security cameras. Hopefully, they caught the asshole who did this."

"I'll contact the building manager and see if I can get a copy of the tapes," Atwater said as he joined them. Taking a card out of his breast pocket, he scribbled a number on it before handing it to Regina. "That's the report number for your insurance company. And if you have any questions or think of anyone who may have done this, the phone number for my department voice mail is on there too. Call me anytime."

Those last three words were said with a hint of suggestiveness, and she wasn't the only one who'd heard it. Frowning, Buck growled lowly and took a step closer to her. Undeterred, the cop just smiled and said, "You take care now, Ms. Vaughn. Goodnight."

As the officer returned to his vehicle in the outside parking lot, Regina turned to face Ryan and Buck. "So, what do I do now? Dad never covered how to change four tires at once."

Despite the situation, both men snorted and chuckled, the tension in them easing a bit. Ryan gestured to the security gate. "Can you plug in your code, so I can bring Mikey's flatbed in? We stopped by on the way over and picked it up." Mikey was their cousin who was an auto mechanic and had his own repair shop about two miles down the road. "He said he's got four tires in this size already in stock. I'll help him replace the flats, and then he'll do an alignment. Buck can take you home now in his truck, and I'll drive yours back to the house when we're done." Well, that explained why Buck was there.

Hell. She really didn't want to go anywhere with Buck right then, but she didn't see a way out of her brother's plan without giving that fact away. "Um . . . okay. Tell Mikey I said thanks for staying late and I'll swing by tomorrow to pay him for everything."

"I doubt he'll worry about that. He knows you're good for it."

Glancing at her SUV, she let out a heavy sigh. "Why would someone do this?"

"Piss anyone off lately, Gi?" Buck asked.

You mean, besides you? Not that he would ever do something so cruel as slashing her tires, no matter how mad he was at her. "No."

"Could your ex-fiancé be this vindictive?"

"No! No, Edward would never do something like this. Besides, he's engaged to Courtney now. I have no idea who would do this. Maybe they thought it was someone else's truck?"

She eyed her brother and Buck, both of whom were staring back at her. Neither of them thought the vandal had gotten the wrong vehicle. Unfortunately, for some unknown reason, she agreed with them. Damn.

twelve

*I*t took about ten minutes for them to get the vehicle loaded onto the flatbed and secured with chains. While Ryan climbed into the cab of the truck, Buck picked up Regina's briefcase and walked with her to the gate. Ryan didn't need her code to get out—the arm would lift as he approached it.

When they reached Buck's Silverado, he opened the passenger door and helped her in before closing it again. He circled around to the driver's side, set her briefcase behind the seat, and got in. As he started the engine, he asked, "Need to make any stops on the way?"

She shook her head. "No, thanks." There was a pause and then, "Actually, on second thought, can we swing by Say Cheez, so I can pick up a pizza? I don't feel like cooking anything tonight and doubt Ryan will want to by the time he gets home."

"Yeah, sure. Call it in, so we don't have to wait long."

Despite her ordering the pizza in advance, they still had to wait a few minutes for the pie to be ready. Buck had parked his truck and gone inside with her, requesting two slices to go for when Regina's order was ready. Selecting a bottle of Coke out of the standing cooler for himself, he also grabbed a root beer and handed it to Regina, knowing it was her favorite. She gave him a faint smile when she accepted it. "Thanks."

He gestured to an empty table near the door. "Let's have a seat while we're waiting."

After she slid into the booth, he sat opposite her and took in her appearance. She looked weary. "Long day?" he asked.

She took a sip of her soda and then nodded. "Yeah, and that was before the four flat tires. Who would do something like that, Buck?"

"Nobody comes to mind?"

"Nobody I can think of. I mean, I'm not someone who runs around making enemies."

No, she wasn't. As her eyes filled with unshed tears, he reached over and grasped her hand. "Hey, it's gonna be all right. Maybe it was a mistake like you said—someone vandalized the wrong vehicle."

Her head shook. "You didn't believe that any more than Ryan did when I said it earlier."

He wasn't going to lie to her and deny it, so he changed the subject. Unfortunately, it wasn't a much better one—at least, not yet. "About the other night—"

"I'm sorry about that."

"What? What are you sorry for? I'm the one who screwed up again."

Her shoulders sagged as a pleading expression stole

across her face. "What are we doing, Buck? I can't go through this again. You hurt me badly seven years ago."

Pulling her hand closer, he gave it a squeeze. "I know I did, and I swear, it was never my intention. I'd never purposely hurt you, baby. It's just . . . God, I want you, Gi. At some point, that summer, I started seeing you as a beautiful, sensual woman and not my best friend's kid sister or even just my own friend. But you were still young, still had so much to see and do. And I was trying to recover from shit from my last tour. I knew if we started something back then, I'd bring you down, and that's the last thing I ever wanted to do. I meant what I said the other night. You're the brightest light in my world, and I'm so afraid the things I've done and seen will make you look at me differently—like I was a monster or something."

"What? I would never—God, Buck, do you think I'm that shallow?'"

"No!" He shook his head. "I'm doing it again. I'm saying the wrong things, and I'm getting you upset. Listen. Can we start over? Can we go on an actual date? I'm attracted to you, Gi, and have been for a long time. I honestly don't think we would've worked back then. It might've been fun for a while, but in the end, we would've wound up hating each other."

"How can—"

"Listen to me. No interrupting, squirt." He smiled to let her know he was teasing her. "That's the past. We've both grown since then. I'm not being deployed to the worst hellholes on Earth anymore, and you've become one helluva woman. One I would really, really like to get to know better. I want our friendship back, and I want to build on it to make it something more. Something good." He squeezed her hand again. "You don't have to answer me tonight. In fact, I don't want you to. Think about it. Sleep on it. Just know that you mean more to me than any woman I've ever known, and I think we could be good together."

When the corners of her mouth ticked upward and she gave his hand a squeeze like he'd done, he knew he'd made his case. Now, he just had to figure out how to tell Ryan he'd be dating the guy's sister.

❧ ❧ ❧ ❧ ❧

"WHERE ARE you going all dressed up?" Ryan asked as Regina walked into the living room wearing a nice red sweater, her favorite boot-cut jeans, and black, low-heeled boots. She'd blown her hair out and added some subtle makeup.

It'd been a few days since the tire slashing incident, and unfortunately, there were a couple of blind spots on the security camera system, which also produced grainy videos. All the police had been able to find on the recordings was someone of unknown gender with a hoodie and gloves on, skirting around in the shadows about an hour before Regina had gone to her vehicle. They'd showed the video to Regina, but she'd been unable to help figure out who the person was. Nothing had happened since, so she was hoping it'd been a random event and wouldn't happen again.

Not wanting to tell Ryan she was going on a date with

his best friend—a conversation she planned on putting off for as long as possible—Regina shrugged and lied. "Out with a few friends for dinner."

He yawned and plopped down on his favorite recliner with the TV remote in his hand. "Glad one of us has energy for a social life. It's not even seven thirty yet, and I'm ready for bed."

Studying him as he flipped up the recliner's footrest, she frowned. He'd changed out of his work clothes into a pair of black sweatpants and a well-worn US Marines T-shirt. Dark circles were visible under his eyes, his black hair was disheveled, as if he'd run his hands through it several times, and a five-o'clock shadow painted his jawline and upper lip. "You do look beat. Are you off tomorrow?" Since it would be Sunday, she hoped he'd take the day off. He'd been working his ass off all week at the resort—so had Buck and Justin and the rest of the staff—getting everything ready for the ski season and the Halloween festivities, which started in a few weeks.

"I'm going to go in for a couple of hours in the morning, but I'll have the afternoon off to lie around and do nothing but watch the Patriot's game."

Hmm. "Why don't we invite Justin, Buck, and Zia over for the game? While you're at work, I can run to the supermarket and grab some beer and food. It's been ages since we've had everyone over for Sunday football."

"Zia's home?"

"Just until Monday. Today's her grandmother's birthday, so she came home last night and doesn't have classes on Monday, so she'll go back to the city then." The two of them had gone out last night for dinner and drinks. She really missed her best friend being so close, but Zia had taken two years off school before going back to get her master's degree in education, and she had one more semester to go.

"Yeah, I'm up for having a few people over for the game. You tell Zia, and I'll send a text to Justin and Buck in a little bit and tell them to come by tomorrow. But right now, all I want to do is watch some TV until I have the strength to make myself something to eat."

She smiled at him. "Got you covered on that, big brother. I needed something to do earlier, so I made Mom's beef stew. It's in the stockpot in the fridge. Just pop a bowlful in the microwave."

His eyes had widened at the words "Mom's beef stew." It'd been their favorite meal growing up, and their mother used to have to chase them out of the kitchen to keep them from eating the entire batch in one night. A few months after their parents had died, Regina had been thrilled when she'd found her mother's recipe for the stew, believing the woman had always just made it from memory. Since then, Regina only made it every few months because it took a lot of prep time and then hours to cook.

"Gi, you're a godsend, you know that?"

"Yeah, well, just don't eat it all tonight. There's plenty for everyone for tomorrow."

He held up one hand and put the other over his heart. "I swear, I'll only have a bowl or two . . . or three, but no more than four."

Laughing, she snatched a small pillow from the couch and threw it at his head. "Idiot."

He caught the pillow easily, and instead of throwing it back at her, tucked it under his head. "Thanks, brat. Now, go have some fun. Flirt with some guys, but only ones I'd approve of. You haven't been on a date since you've been back in Largo Ridge." His eyes narrowed. "Or have you and you just don't want me checking them out?"

Sidestepping his question, she grabbed her purse. "Haven't been on a date in a while? That's the pot calling the kettle black. When was the last time you went out with a woman?"

He rolled his eyes. "Fine. I won't ask about your love life and you don't ask about mine. But if it's something serious, we'll let the other know. Agreed?"

Okay, that gave her some more time to see where this thing with Buck was going before she had to tell Ryan anything. "Agreed."

thirteen

*A*fter waiting patiently for a few minutes in front of a little steakhouse in Bellewood, Buck was relieved to see Regina's SUV pull into the parking lot. He'd been worried she might've gotten cold feet about going out on an actual, pre-planned date with him. He was also still concerned the police hadn't been able to figure out who'd slashed her tires. Some people had a lot of enemies, but Regina Vaughn could only count on one hand anyone she'd even remotely pissed off lately. The list included her ex-fiancé, her former in-laws-to-be, some guy from the CPA office who'd lost the LRSR contract, and Margo Shaw, who Buck had run into the other day. She'd hit on him again, and he'd turned her down—again. However, Regina swore she couldn't imagine any of those people being so vindictive that they'd sneak into the parking garage and slash her tires. The police had been able to get alibis from each of them, so they'd all been ruled out. That didn't mean that any of them couldn't have hired someone to do the deed.

As Regina approached, Buck's grin and heart grew. With twinkling eyes, she smiled back at him. The woman was so damn beautiful, she almost brought him to his knees. Neither of them had wanted to risk going out to a restaurant in Largo Ridge and having anyone spot them. While they'd had dinner together before, just the two of them, most people who knew them wouldn't have suspected a thing was going on, since they'd been friends for most of their lives. However, with the sexual tension that was now noticeably arcing between them, surely someone would realize the dynamics of their relationship had changed and rumors would spread like wildfire. While they knew they'd have to tell Ryan sooner or later, they wanted to make sure what they felt for each other wasn't going to fizzle out after a few dates. Longtime crushes could either become an amazing reality or they could've been misinterpreted and not turn out as good as the participants had hoped for.

"Hi," she said shyly as she stopped in front of him. A blush appeared on her upper chest and spread to her neck and cheeks. Buck couldn't remember the last time a woman had blushed like that for him without him hitting on her for a brief roll in the sack. His body reacted accordingly, with his cock twitching.

They hadn't seen each other since Wednesday night. After getting their pizza, Buck had driven her back to her house, where he'd gone inside and had dinner with her while waiting for Ryan to return. He hadn't felt comfortable leaving her alone, without a vehicle, knowing someone had intentionally slashed her tires. They'd passed the time talking, like they'd done the night they'd gone to the Red Door Saloon. As the evening had progressed, she'd seemed more at ease with him. He'd bumbled through his explanation of how and why he'd fucked up with her, and thankfully, she'd forgiven him. At least, she acted as if she had. He just prayed that was all behind them.

The past few days, they'd talked over the phone during their lunch hours and after work and had texted in between. It'd been the highlight of his days when his phone would jingle with the ringtone and alert tone he'd assigned to her name.

Instead of saying anything in response to her greeting, he cupped her jaw and lowered his mouth to hers. He smiled when she rose up on her toes, meeting him halfway. Keeping in mind they were out in public, he kissed her tenderly, fighting the urge to plunge his tongue inside her mouth and mimic what his cock wanted to do to her pussy.

After a few moments, he lifted his head and gazed at her adoringly. "Hi, back."

She giggled as he took her hand and tucked it into the crook of his arm before leading her to the restaurant's door and opening it for her. She was his princess, and he would treat her as such every chance he could.

❄ ❄ ❄ ❄ ❄

REGINA COULDN'T BELIEVE she was on a date—an actual date—with Buck. Despite her years of hurt, she'd still fantasized about the man. There was something about him—pheromones or something—that just drew her to him like a bear to honey.

As they followed the waitress to a table, Regina didn't miss the looks of appreciation Buck was getting from several women in the place. A twinge of jealousy disappeared the moment she felt his hand on her lower back, as if he were grounding her to him. She knew she was taking a huge risk by accepting his apology and trying to put all the negatives in the past, so they could start fresh. But, while her mind warned her to be wary, her heart and the rest of her body knew what they wanted —the man she could all too easily admit she was falling in love with.

Even though Buck had told her Justin had figured out the two of them had feelings for each other and had encouraged him to ask Regina out, no one else knew, as far as she could tell. She hadn't even told Zia or any of the other girlfriends she'd reconnected with since returning to Largo Ridge that she was going on a date with Buck. For now, she wanted to keep it a secret—maybe because she wanted him all to herself or maybe because she was protecting her heart. If this thing between them failed, she wouldn't have to see the looks of pity or "I told you so" directed at her.

They'd barely ordered their drinks when her cell phone vibrated on the unoccupied seat next to her where she'd also placed her purse. She glanced at the screen and saw her brother's name. Not wanting to lie to him again about where she'd been going tonight, she rejected the call. A few seconds later, it vibrated again, and she frowned.

Over his menu, Buck asked, "Who is it?"

"Ryan." She gave him a worried look. "Do you think he knows we're out together?"

"I doubt it, since my phone isn't blowing up too. Answer it."

Taking a deep breath, she picked up the phone and accepted the call. "Hello?"

"Where are you?"

At her brother's sharp, anxious tone, her gaze flew to Buck's. "I'm out with friends, why?"

"Damn it, Gi. Where?"

"At Chico's." It was a TexMex restaurant about halfway between Largo Ridge and Bellewood. She wasn't sure why she'd lied to him again, but it was too late to take it back. "What's wrong?"

"You're with friends?"

"Yes. Ryan, you're scaring me. What's wrong?"

A few tables of diners glanced her way after her voice had risen above normal. When Buck reached across the table and gestured for her to hand over the phone, she shook her head and listened to her brother.

"I'm calling Buck to come and get you and follow you home. Someone threw a brick through the living room window."

Her eyes widened in shock. "Wha—"

"I have the police responding, and I want you home safely. Do not leave there until Buck gets there, okay?" When she hesitated, his tone became more urgent. "Gi, do you understand me? You stay there until Buck gets there."

"O-okay. Yeah, I promise. Ryan, are you all right?"

"Yeah. I'll explain everything when you get home. Be careful."

The call disconnected, and three seconds later, Buck's phone vibrated in his hand. He answered immediately in a low voice. "Hey, Ry. What's up?" He listened for a moment, his gaze on her face, then said, "Yeah, I can go get her. What's wrong . . . uh-huh . . . shit. All right. We'll be there in a bit. I'll follow her home . . . yeah, I got it covered, bro. Stay safe."

"What did he tell you?" Regina asked, as fear coursed through her body. She had a feeling Ryan hadn't told her everything.

Not answering her, Buck flagged their middle-aged waitress who'd been at the bar, probably waiting for their drink order. When she hurried over, he explained they had an emergency and had to leave. "Could you get me the check?"

She peeked over her shoulder toward the bar, then turned back to Buck. "No worries. He hasn't gotten your drinks yet, so I'll just cancel them."

Standing, he gave her a terse smile. "Thanks. I'm sorry about this."

"It's really no problem. I hope everything's okay," she added, giving Regina an encouraging look.

"Thank you." Regina had also gotten to her feet and gathered her things.

After the waitress left them to go cancel their drink order, Buck threw a twenty-dollar bill on the table, then gestured for Regina to proceed him toward the exit. Not wanting to disturb the other patrons any more than they'd already done, she waited until they were outside before she bombarded Buck with questions. "What did he tell you? What else is wrong besides a brick being thrown through the window?" As if that wasn't bad enough. "Was he hurt?"

Grasping her elbow, he led her across the lot to where she'd parked her SUV. "No, he was in the kitchen when it happened. He ran outside, but whoever threw it had already taken off. He's worried it's related to your tires getting slashed."

"What?"

"That's all I know, Gi. He said he'd fill us in when we got there." They reached her truck, and he helped her into the driver's seat before cupping her chin and turning her head toward him. "Are you okay to drive?" When she nodded, he hesitated a moment, studying her face. "Okay. I'm going to follow you there. Wait for me to get my truck before you pull out and be careful you don't lose me on the way. I'll stay close behind."

"O-okay."

He leaned in and brushed his lips across hers. "It'll be okay, Gi. I won't let anything happen to you."

fourteen

*A*s two patrolmen and a detective from the Largo Ridge Police Department left, after taking some photos and a statement from Ryan, Regina pulled the vacuum, broom, and dustpan out from where they were stored in a closet in the hall. Justin and one of the maintenance guys from the resort, Tim Keller, had driven up a short while ago with several sheets of plywood and some tools. With Buck and Ryan's help, they were removing pieces of the broken glass that'd remained stuck into the plateglass window frame before shoring up the opening with the plywood. Ryan would call the glass repair shop in town and get a replacement put in as soon as possible. Hopefully, it would only be a day or two.

Regina was still shaking from the incident. What Ryan hadn't told her until she and Buck had arrived home was that there'd been a message taped to the brick that'd been thrown through the window and had also been taken as evidence. A white piece of paper with black marker lettering had announced, "You're next, bitch!"

As Buck had mentioned, Ryan had been in the kitchen, reheating the beef stew, when he'd heard the crash. In slippered feet, he'd run out the front door, without thinking twice about it, but the suspect had disappeared into the night. The patrolmen had knocked on several of the neighbors' doors, but no one had seen or heard anything. There was enough distance between the houses for someone who lived right next door to not be able to hear the glass breaking, especially if they had a TV or radio on.

After discovering there had been a previous vandalizing of Regina's tires, the patrolmen had called in a detective to investigate. The responding detective had been Heath Cobb, who'd been a year younger in school than Ryan and his friends, but they'd all played football and baseball together. Unfortunately, Heath wasn't optimistic about getting any fingerprints off the piece of paper, but he'd said he would at least try when he got back to the police station. He'd warned Regina to be careful and to report any other incidents or anyone acting suspiciously to the police. Ryan had assured him that he, Buck, and Justin would make sure she remained safe.

By the time the men were finished putting up the plywood and a sheet of heavy plastic over it to prevent any drafts, Regina had swept and then vacuumed up all the pieces of glass she could find. It'd scattered everywhere—onto the couch, Ryan's recliner, the coffee and end tables, the carpet, and even out into the hallway and foyer. Tomorrow, in the daylight, she'd give everything another round of cleaning. She and Ryan would have to wear slippers or shoes at all times until she was certain there were no slivers that'd escaped the suck of the vacuum.

When Ryan entered the house with the others, he strode toward her and gave her a hug. "You okay, Gi?"

With her arms around him, she patted his back. She still had a few tremors of fear and anxiety racing through her, which had started on the drive home, but the worst of it was over. "Yeah, I guess. I just wish I knew why someone is after me."

"So do I. And when I find the son of a bitch—"

Justin slapped him on the shoulder as he passed them. "We'll help you bury the body."

Regina groaned and let go of her brother. "Justin, don't say that."

"Why not? It's the truth."

"Because if you get caught, and I get subpoenaed, I don't want to have to lie under oath that I didn't know anything about it."

All four men stilled and stared at her for a moment. It was Buck who burst out laughing first, followed by the others. "Atta girl."

With the mood changed and lightened, as she'd hoped it would be, she asked, "Is anyone hungry? I can heat up the beef stew."

"Is that your mom's beef stew?" Justin asked, rubbing a hand over his stomach. "If it is, I'd love some."

"Hell, yeah," Buck chimed in.

An hour later, everyone had eaten their fill of the stew, leaving only a few helpings in the pot. Justin and Tim took their leave after Buck and Ryan said they'd take care of the dishes. Meanwhile, Regina went to her bedroom

SAMANTHA A. COLE

and changed into a pair of sweatpants and a long-sleeved T-shirt. By the time she returned to the kitchen, everything had been cleaned or put away.

Buck's gaze fell on her, and she could see the hunger in his eyes when he seemed to realize she'd taken her bra off too. But then he glanced at Ryan, whose back was to them as he was lifting the full bag out of the trash can. Sighing, with a disappointed expression, Buck said, "It's been a long night. I should be getting home. I'll talk to you tomorrow?"

Although his question had been directed at Regina, Ryan had assumed it'd been meant for him and responded, "Yup. Patriots are playing at four. Don't be late."

He winked at Regina. "Yeah, I don't think you have to worry about that."

* * * * * *

JUST AFTER EIGHT on Tuesday evening, Regina followed Buck into his house. Each time she was there, she couldn't believe how much work he'd done since purchasing it. She hadn't seen it back then, but Ryan had mentioned the house had been in sore need of repairs when Buck had first moved in. From the look of the kitchen, en suite bath, and principal bedroom, which hadn't been touched yet, she would have to agree. With the help of his friends, Buck had already replaced all the old walls and ceilings with sheetrock in the living room, dining room, hallways, and two spare bedrooms that were on the second floor. He was going to finish off one of the latter before temporarily moving his bed in there while he tackled the largest bedroom.

A full bath off the upstairs hallway had already received a makeover, with beautiful, walnut cabinets, a black marble countertop, black and white tiles on the floor, and a white bathtub, toilet, and sink with silver fixtures. The walls had been painted a soft gray, and the countertop accessories and towels were burgundy and white. That'd been the first room to be redone, since he'd had no desire to use it the way it'd been any longer than necessary.

"Watch your step," he told her. Long lengths of crown molding had been laid out and piled up against one wall of the hallway leading to the kitchen. "Those are going up next. Then on Monday, the guys are coming to lay down the new wooden floors."

"You're not doing that yourself?"

"Nah . . . I have enough backbreaking work to do. I hired a company to do the wood floors. I'll be doing the tile in the foyer, kitchen, and the half-bath down here though."

In the kitchen, which had seen better days, Buck set the pizza and six-pack of beer they'd picked up on the way home on the table. Meanwhile, Regina took off her coat and began to gather the paper plates and napkins they needed from one of the cabinets. It was much later than she usually ate dinner, and she was starving. He'd picked her up at her house after work, and they'd gone to a furniture store to select a few things.

When she'd met up with everyone at the resort for their monthly meeting, the subject of Buck's lack of available furniture had come up. Trying not to sound too interested, she'd offered to go with him to look for a few pieces, like a couch, recliner, tables, and TV cabinet for his sixty-inch widescreen to sit on. A dinette set had also been needed to replace the folding table and chairs they were currently using in the kitchen. Regina had been surprised when Ryan had said it was a great idea for her to go with Buck because she had a far better sense of style than any of the men. Buck had given her a covert wink, clearly acknowledging the sly trick to be able to spend time with him, since they still hadn't told Ryan they were dating.

Taking a large bite of his pizza, Buck moaned in delight as the sauce and cheese tantalized his taste buds. Around a mouthful, he said, "God, I didn't realize how hungry I was."

"It's been a long day."

Under the table, he ran his sock-covered foot up the outside of her leg. "Thanks for coming with me today. I would've been overwhelmed with the choices if you weren't there."

"Are you sure you like everything?"

Nodding, he chewed another bite, then swallowed. "Absolutely. Everything is good-looking, functional, and comfortable—and it doesn't look all mismatched like the stuff from my old apartment. After Christmas, we'll go back and find a dining room set and furniture for my bedroom. The spare bedrooms can wait until spring." He was currently using the mismatched bedroom set he'd brought back to Largo Ridge with him from Massachusetts. His huge TV was in there too. What little else he had was currently in a unit at a nearby storage facility, while he worked on the rest of the house. Apparently, the loveseat and recliner he'd had for years were worn to the point he'd made the decision to toss them instead of putting them in the nice, new living room.

"Sounds good to me."

They chatted about other normal, everyday things as they ate until they were both full. After they cleaned up, Buck grabbed her arms and pulled her into an embrace. "Thanks again for lending a hand tonight. I kind of like the fact you helped pick out the furniture for my house. At least when you move in with me, I won't have to worry about you not liking it."

Regina stilled as she stared up at him. Had she heard him right? "When I move in with you?"

He arched a brow and frowned. "Should I have said *if* you move in with me?"

Thinking about it a moment, she realized the idea of moving in with Buck didn't make her anxious like it'd been with Edward. With a seductive grin, she slid her hands up and down his muscular chest. "*When* works for me . . . on one condition."

He cupped her ass. "Yeah, what's that?"

"Well, I haven't tried out the bed yet. I'll have to see if it's comfortable or not."

A sexy leer appeared on his face, fanning the flames of desire roaring to life within her. "Oh, I think we can take care of that right now."

Without another word, he leaned down, put his arm behind her knees, and swooped her up, cradling her against his chest. Regina squeaked then laughed as he carried her down the hall to the stairs and up to the second floor. She took advantage of her current position to nuzzle his neck and ears, licking and nibbling on his skin. Inhaling deeply, she let his aftershave tantalize her nose. It was the same delicious scent he'd worn all those years ago. The one she'd never forgotten.

When they reached his bedroom, Buck kicked the door shut and relaxed his hold on Regina until she slid down his body and back onto her feet again. Cupping her jaw, Buck lowered his head and took possession of her mouth. He sucked her plump bottom lip between his, then ran his tongue over it, drawing a moan of desire from her lungs.

While he backed her up toward the bed, Regina grasped the hem of his sweater and lifted. Buck stopped kissing her, so he could help her rid him of the garment and then her own top. His big hands cupped her restrained breasts, running his thumbs over the pebbled nipples with just the thin material of the lacy bra she wore between them. His gaze roamed her chest before lifting to her face. "God, you're beautiful."

Without giving her a chance to respond past a blush, his lips met hers again in a punishing kiss. She opened for him without hesitation, enjoying the slide of his tongue against hers. He pulled her body flush against his, and they fit like two pieces of a puzzle. His erection was straining against the fly of his jeans, and she felt it twitch against her abdomen.

His skin was hot and smooth against hers, and she moaned in protest when he pulled away a few inches. His eyes searched her face. "I don't want to rush you, baby. We don't have to—"

"Shh." Regina placed her fingers over his mouth. "You're not rushing me. I want this, Buck. I know this boyfriend/girlfriend thing is new for us, but, honestly, I've been dreaming of being with you like this for years." It was one of the main reasons she hadn't been able to marry Edward. How could she when her fantasies were filled with the man standing in front of her? The man she was in love with. She couldn't tell him that—not yet—but she knew deep in her heart and soul that Buck was the one she wanted to spend the rest of her life with . . . starting now.

Going up on her tiptoes, she settled her mouth over his, bringing them back to where they'd been a few moments ago. Running her hands over his torso, she delighted in feeling his muscles quiver under her touch. Buck kissed along her jawline to the sensitive spot under her ear. "I want to spend hours worshiping your sweet body."

She giggled as she rubbed against him like a cat. "I want to let you."

Her hands slid down to the button of his jeans and made quick work of it, along with the zipper. When she tried to slip her fingers under the waistband of his boxer briefs, Buck caught her wrists before she could touch him further and wrapped them around his neck. "If you do that, sweetheart, this'll be over before I get you naked."

As she hugged him to her, he devoured her mouth again, then dropped his hands to her jeans and before she realized it, he was pushing the pants and her underwear down her legs. Lifting her feet, she was able to rid herself of both garments seconds before Buck lowered her to the bed.

As she reclined onto the mattress, Buck kissed, sucked, and licked his way down her body, laving her nipples for a few moments before going lower. Goose bumps skittered across her skin as she whimpered with need. The closer he got to the apex of her thighs, the harder her heart was pounding and she was gasping for air. She spread her legs wider as he sank to his knees beside the bed. "Please, Buck!"

"Mmm. I love to hear you beg." He ran his tongue along the crease of her right hip and then the left. But before she could demand he stop teasing her, his mouth closed over her clit and sucked. Regina's pelvis lurched upward at the delicious shockwave that coursed through her, and she cried out for more.

Buck used his fingers to part her folds and then he feasted on her. Regina squirmed, panted, and pleaded as he drove her desire higher and higher, alternating between her slit and her clitoris. Every so often his heavy eyelids would lift, and his gaze would meet hers. The raging storm of passion in his eyes was something she'd never seen before in any of the few lovers she'd had over the years—none of whom could have prepared her for a tempest named Buck.

His tongue delved into her, then shifted to lash at her clit as he eased one and then two fingers inside her. Regina fidgeted under his ministrations, trying to get closer. Her orgasm was right there, just out of reach. She grabbed onto a handful of his hair, and Buck growled but didn't let up his assault. He found the spot inside her, the one that had her quivering. He stroked it several times, then bit down gently on her clit. That was all her body could handle as she screamed her release. Her back bowed as her hands twisted, one still in his hair, the other clutching the comforter. Pleasure roared through her in waves of ecstasy until she sagged into the mattress, floating down from the intense high.

Grinning like a loon, Buck pushed up onto his knees and wiped his sopping wet chin, then licked his fingers. "I plan on having you for dessert every night from now on, baby."

He crawled up onto the bed and kissed her, his tongue sweeping inside her mouth. She could taste herself on him, something she'd never enjoyed before now. Combined with Buck's unique flavor, it was different this time and she couldn't get enough of it.

Pushing up onto one hand and his knees, Buck reached over and opened the drawer to his nightstand, pulling out a box of condoms. Regina hadn't expected the relief she felt when she realized it was a new, unopened box. She hadn't wanted to think about whom Buck had been with before her if there'd been one or more of the tiny packages missing from the box. She wasn't naive enough to think he hadn't been with many women over the years, but she hoped none of them had been in this bedroom with him.

Opening the box, Buck retrieved a foil package and quickly donned the condom. Then he was back on top of her. "Put your legs around me."

She did as she was told, digging her heels into his ass,

urging him to enter her. She felt the tip of his cock ease inside of her. She was still slick from her orgasm and it only took him a few short thrusts to bottom out. Regina felt so full, it took a moment for her body to adjust to Buck's girth.

"Okay, baby?"

Regina nodded and lifted her pelvis. "Yes, please move!"

His mouth settled on hers again as his hips set a torturously slow pace. Regina moaned and ran her hands over every inch of his skin she could reach. When Buck changed the angle of his thrusts, she cried out as he hit her G-spot over and over again. Liquid heat rushed through her veins as Buck increased his pace. As the pressure building within her threatened to explode, she dug her nails into his back. This time, when she went over the edge, she took him with her. His shouts of ecstasy reverberated throughout the bedroom.

As they lay there, completely spent and sated, Regina knew she was finally where she belonged.

fifteen

*S*ated, Buck lay on his back, with Regina cuddled against his side, her head on his shoulder. He'd pulled the bedsheet over their legs and lower torsos, leaving her gorgeous breasts exposed and crushed against him. His fingers caressed her upper arm. He'd figured sex with her would be amazing, but it'd been more than that —mind-blowing was the only way he could think to describe it right then. Never had he felt so completed by a woman, until her.

All those years he'd wasted when he could've had her in his bed. But as he thought about that for a moment, he realized he'd done the right thing seven years ago. Neither of them had been ready for this. She'd been too young to be a soldier's girlfriend, and the long, hard deployments would've destroyed them. No, he'd definitely done the right thing, and he had no trouble thinking up ways to make up for all the lost time. Now that he had her in his bed, he wasn't sure he ever wanted to let her out of it.

That brought up a problem though. A big one.

Buck was seeing a psychiatrist once a week to help him deal with his PTSD, but after trying several recommended drugs on the market, which had side effects such as severe depression, loss of appetite and sex drive, and mind fog, he'd refused to take them anymore. That meant he was still dealing with one or two flashbacks per week while he was awake and having nightmares more often than not. There was no way he could risk falling asleep in the same bed as Regina—not when there was a chance he'd be fighting for his life—at least his subconscious would think he was. He'd be kicking and throwing punches, and just the thought of doing that with Regina by his side, aware of the horrors he was reliving, made him sick to his stomach.

"What's wrong?" she asked, running her hand up and down his bare chest in a soothing manner.

He set his hand on top of hers, stilling it. "We have to talk about something."

"Okaaaay."

The wariness in that one word had him shifting and glancing down at her. Shit. Her gaze was filled with worry. He could imagine all the different questions running through her mind. He placed a gentle kiss on her furrowed brow. "No, I'm not going to take off running again. I don't regret what we just did. Yes, I loved every minute of it and can't wait to do it again. And you're the most beautiful woman I know—sexiest too. Did I cover everything? Any other concerns?"

Her smile was back, and she lifted her chin, silently asking for a kiss. Of course, he obliged her. Once she settled her head back on his shoulder again, she said, "Yes, you covered everything. But that means you want to talk about something else I'm not aware of."

Taking a deep breath, he let it out slowly. "I told you about my PTSD, right?"

"Yes, a little bit. I figured you'd talk about it more when you were ready."

He snorted. "I don't think anyone is ever ready to really talk about it, but there are times it's necessary. Anyway, I get flashbacks when I'm awake and nightmares when I'm asleep, although sometimes, I can't tell them apart. I do have more issues when I'm asleep though. Which is what I wanted to talk to you about. As much as I love having you in my bed, I won't be able to sleep with you—I mean fall asleep with you. I can't risk getting caught up in a nightmare and punching and kicking with you next to me. You also can't approach me if I'm having a nightmare because, in my mind, I'm not here, Gi—I'm somewhere else, somewhere really bad. You can't try to shake me awake or anything because I'll probably swing at you. It would kill me if I hurt you like that.

"So, whenever you sleep over, which I'm hoping you'll do someday soon, after you fall asleep, I'll go sleep on the couch that's coming. Then, in the morning, I'll slip back into bed with you and wake you up—nice and slow." He grinned with those last few words, trying to lighten the mood that always accompanied conversations concerning his PTSD.

"Okay."

His eyebrows shot up. "Okay?"

She nodded. "Yes, it's okay. Am I happy about sleeping in this big bed alone? No. Do I understand your reasoning? Of course I do, Buck. I know if I forced you to sleep with me, you wouldn't actually fall asleep because you'd be afraid of hurting me, and that wouldn't be fair to you. I hope it won't always be like that, but whatever you need to do to get you through the days and nights, I'm willing to support you. I'm not going anywhere. But I also wouldn't object to you bringing me breakfast in bed, every once in a while, before you slip back in and wake me up—nice and slow."

In that moment, Buck fell the rest of the way for Regina Vaughn. He was completely and utterly in love with her—he just wasn't ready to tell her that yet.

⬧ ⬧ ⬧ ⬧ ⬧

BUCK COULDN'T REMEMBER the last time he'd been this nervous. It wasn't every day a guy told his best friend he was in love with the man's sister and he was sleeping with her. Well, not exactly sleeping, but he wasn't going to come right out and say the three-letter S-word. Buck knew how queasy he felt when his sister and brother-in-law got all lusty-eyed for each other in his presence. No guy wanted to think about his sister having sex. It ranked right up there with imagining his parents doing the dirty deed—nauseating.

Striding into the maintenance building, he said hello to Ryan's secretary as he passed her and entered the open door to his friend's office, closing it behind him. Ryan was sitting behind his desk with a stack of papers that looked like invoices in front of him. He glanced up. "Hey, what's up?"

Dropping onto the only guest chair in the room, Buck leaned forward, resting his elbows on his thighs. "Got a few minutes?"

Ryan tossed the pen he'd been using on top of the papers and leaned back. "Sure."

Taking a deep breath, Buck let it out slowly. Suddenly, the chair seemed too confining. He stood and paced back and forth while Ryan's gaze followed him. "I don't know how to say this. I mean, I've been trying all week to find the words. It's . . . it's just really hard."

"What are you talking about, Buck?" Concern laced his tone and bloomed on his face.

Taking the bull by the horns, Buck stopped in front of the desk and blurted, "I'm dating Gi."

Ryan froze and blinked a few times, then burst out laughing, the loud sound filling the room and bouncing off the walls. "Oh, crap! For a moment there, I thought you said you're dating Gi."

Rolling his eyes, Buck crossed his arms and frowned. "I'm not kidding, Ry. I'm dating your sister."

The room filled with testosterone-edged tension as Ryan's laughter died down and he scowled. "No, you're not. No fucking way are you dating Regina."

"Listen, hear me out before you get all pissed and start swinging at me."

"*Before* I get pissed? There is no *before*! Because I'm already fucking there, dude. You. Are. *Not*. Dating. My sister."

"She's an adult, Ry. She can date anyone she wants. This isn't something new . . . at least, not for me. I've liked her for a long time now but never acted on it, except a kiss years ago. I fucked up and hurt her—not intentionally, and I really regret it. I was in a bad place, in between deployments, and didn't want to pull her into that. She's had it in her head for all these years that she was the problem. We've talked about it recently and got past it. We've been out on a few dates and knew we couldn't and shouldn't hide it from you anymore. I care for her a lot, man. Hell, I'm in love with her."

Ryan jumped to his feet, sending his chair crashing into the wall, and leaned on his hands on the desktop, glaring at him. Buck half expected the guy to vault over the desk and tackle him. "What the hell, Buck? My goddamn sister? You're fucking Gi?"

He growled, anger that matched Ryan's flaring in his eyes as he took a warning step toward his friend. "Watch your mouth, Ry. This isn't some random chick I'm having a short fling with here."

"No, it's *not* some random chick—it's my fucking sister!"

"Who is the last person in the world I would intentionally hurt. Damn it. This didn't just happen out of nowhere. She and I have been dancing around this thing between us for years. I thought I would stop wanting her, needing her, after she got engaged. I thought I could forget about how I felt about her. But it didn't happen. I love her, Ry. I really love her. Would you rather her be with some jackass you don't know or like, or someone you know almost as well as you know yourself? A man who cares deeply for her, who knows how special she is to you? Someone who will treat her like she's the most precious thing on Earth?"

Ryan exhaled heavily. As the breath left his lungs, it seemed to take some of his ire with it. The tension in his arms, shoulders, and jaw eased. After a moment, he grabbed the arm of his chair, rolled it back into position, and sat down again. "Jesus." He ran a hand down his face. "You couldn't have given a guy some kind of warning before throwing that at him on a Monday fucking morning?"

It was a rhetorical question. The wheels in Ryan's brain appeared to be spinning, contemplating, and Buck gave him a few moments of silence to gather his thoughts. He dropped into the guest chair again and waited his friend out.

Pinning him with a glare, with far less heat than before, Ryan said, "You better not hurt her, Buck. You're my best friend, but she's my sister. Don't make me beat the living shit out of you."

He snorted. "As if you could. Listen. The last thing I would ever do is hurt her intentionally. But whether or not this thing between us works out, every couple has their arguments. I don't want you throwing down with me because she's upset I left the toilet seat up or something."

With that, his friend let out a chuckle. "I get it. No throw downs over toilet seats." He shook his head. "My sister? Really?"

A smile spread across Buck's face for the first time that morning. "Really."

sixteen

*R*egina wasn't certain what had awoken her, but it took her a moment to remember she wasn't in her own bed. After making love, then having dinner, followed by another round of sex that'd been much raunchier and orgasmic than the first, she'd dozed off in Buck's arms. She hated that he was afraid to let down his guard and fall asleep next to her, but she understood his reasoning. Maybe over time, he'd be more comfortable and find that sleeping with her reduced his nightmares.

She wished his therapist could do more for him or there was a new drug that could help without all the nasty side effects, but no matter what, she wasn't going to let his flashbacks and nightmares drive her away. He meant too much to her for her to not want to stand by him through thick or thin.

Sitting up, she thought about the wedding vows she was supposed to have taken months ago. *". . . for better, for worse, for richer, for poorer, in sickness and in health, to love and to cherish, till death do us part . . ."* While she hadn't been able to say those words to Edward, she knew in her heart she could say them to Buck. Whether it happened tomorrow or five years from now, she would still be willing to take those vows.

An odd sound from outside the bedroom caught her attention. "Buck?" she called out softly but received no answer. She tried again, a little louder. "Buck? Is that you?"

When she still didn't get a response, she tossed the sheets off her naked body and stood. Glancing around, she spotted the T-shirt he'd worn earlier and pulled it on over her head. It was several sizes too big on her, but she got a kick out of wearing it. A glance at the digital clock on the nightstand, which lit up the room just enough for her not to freak at the darkness, read 2:21 a.m. She tucked her feet into a fuzzy pair of white slippers Buck had gotten for her, not wanting her walking around barefoot or in stocking feet while the interior of the house was still being worked on.

Another sound—a man's anguished voice crying out— had her hurrying to the closed door and yanking it open. Again, she heard the voice and, that time, was able to determine it was Buck's.

Regina rushed out to the living room and slid to a stop on the recently installed wood flooring with its highly buffed varnish, her heart and gut clenching. Buck was lying on the new couch, his eyes shut, and his face contorted, as if in pain. His body was writhing. The blanket on top of him was entwined between and around his legs, preventing him from kicking his feet free, and a pillow was on the floor.

"No! Adkins, get down!" Sweat poured off him as he barked out orders to people only his mind could see. "Corpsman! Man down! Jeffries, watch the left flank!" He grabbed the back cushion of the couch and twisted it in his fist. "Incoming!"

Regina couldn't watch it anymore. She stepped forward, cautiously. "Buck! Wake up! It's me, Regina."

She didn't get through to him. His voice went from mumbles to shouts and back again. He was fighting an invisible enemy—although it probably seemed real to him in his unconscious state.

Taking a few more steps, she closed the distance between them, hesitating only a moment before moving around to the other side of the glass coffee table they'd bought with all the other new furniture. With a trembling hand, she reached out and shook his shoulder. "Buck! Wake up!"

His eyes flew open, and there was a feral look in them. In what seemed like a fraction of a second, he grasped her wrist with one hand and thrust his other at her torso. Regina's feet came out from underneath her as pain bloomed in her diaphragm. She lost her breath as she went reeling backward and crashed on top of the coffee table. The glass broke under the weight and shock, dropping her to the ground in severe agony as her back was sliced open. Her head slammed against the floor, adding to her pain. Black and white dots flashed in front of her eyes.

It'd all happened so fast, she hadn't even screamed, and

now, as she struggled to breathe, it was impossible to say anything.

"Gi! Oh my God!" Buck had gotten to his feet and was standing over her, horror contorting his features as he realized what'd happened. "Gi, are you okay? Shit! Don't . . . don't move."

Regina's head swam, and she closed her eyes to fight back the pain, double vision, and nausea assaulting her.

"Yes! I need an ambulance at . . ." He rattled off his address, fear and shock lacing his tone. "My girlfriend is hurt—please hurry! Oh my God, Gi! I'm so sorry! It's all my fault. I-I didn't mean it! Oh, God, please tell them to hurry!"

HIS CELL PHONE ringing pulled Ryan out of a deep sleep. He blinked a few times until his eyes adjusted to the dark bedroom. He had no idea what time it was, but it was still the middle of the night. No sunlight peeked in from behind the shades covering the two windows in his bedroom.

As the annoying ringing continued, Ryan groaned and turned onto his side, reaching out for the offensive device on his nightstand. He glanced at the screen. *Largo Ridge Hospital.* That brought him fully awake and sitting up. He hit the connect button, and his voice was raspy when he said, "Hello?"

"Ryan! You have to help Buck! They arrested him!"

Regina was hysterical, her voice screeching to the point he had to pull the phone a little further from his ear.

"Gi! Calm down. What're you talking about? Where are you?"

"Please, you have to tell them it was all my fault. I shouldn't have—"

"Damn it, Gi, what happened?"

She began sobbing, making it harder for him to understand her. He grabbed his pants from the floor, not even recalling getting out of the bed. Suddenly, a male voice came on the line. "Vaughn? It's Josh Boyd."

"Josh? What the fuck is going on? Where's my sister?" The man had gone to high school with Ryan and his friends and was a detective on the Largo Ridge PD.

"She's at the ER. She's okay, just banged up. I need you to come down here."

His heart pounding, he searched for the shirt he'd removed earlier, then remembered he'd tossed it in the hamper in the bathroom. He yanked open the second drawer of his dresser and pulled out a clean T-shirt. "What did she mean Buck's been arrested? What the hell happened?"

A long sigh came over the line, as if the man hated what he was about to say. "He was arrested on a domestic violence charge. I'll explain it all when you get here."

"Fuck! I'm on my way."

Twelve minutes later, Ryan whipped his truck into an empty parking space in the hospital's ER lot. Leaping from the driver's seat, he slammed the door shut and ran toward the building. Having been to the emergency room several times over the years, for himself or his friends and family members, he ignored the doors to the reception area and waiting room, heading to the ambulance entrance instead.

The double doors automatically separated when he stepped on the rubber matting covering a sensor plate in front of them. A second set of double doors opened, but before he could walk through them, he was stopped by a tall, bald security guard, who stepped in his way. "Sorry, sir, you need to enter through the waiting room."

Ryan pointed beyond the guard's shoulder. "My sister's in there—"

The man was about to argue with him when Josh Boyd appeared behind him. "Craig, it's okay. I called him. You can let him in."

Craig nodded and moved out of the way. "Sure thing, Detective."

Ryan shook the hand Josh had extended toward him. "Where is she?"

"In the suture room, but I want to talk to you, first." When an ambulance pulled up outside, Josh grasped Ryan's upper arm and moved him into an unoccupied room near the entrance. It appeared to be where the police and EMTs wrote their reports.

"What the hell happened?"

Crossing his arms, Josh leaned against the wall. The man stood six four and was solid muscle. With a short, blond crewcut, he was dressed in a navy-blue polo shirt, with LARGO RIDGE PD and the department's shield embroidered on the left side of his chest, tan cargo pants, and black, rubber-soled shoes. A holstered 9mm handgun was strapped to his belt over his right hip. His ice-blue eyes were sharp and assessing.

"According to patrol, they found Regina on the floor. She'd fallen backward onto a glass coffee table, and it broke, slicing up her back." When Ryan stiffened, frowned, and clenched his fist, the detective held up a hand. "Relax. They're mostly superficial cuts, but there are about two or three that will need a few stitches. Nothing too deep. Anyway, Regina told the guys who responded that Buck was sleeping on the couch and was having a nightmare. She tried to wake him up, and he reacted by shoving her back. She lost her balance and fell. Apparently, the T-shirt she'd been wearing had helped protect her from the injuries being worse. Now, I haven't interviewed her yet. I wanted to wait until you got here to get your opinion on whether she's telling the truth or she's trying to cover for him and this was something along the lines of a domestic violence thing."

Not sure what to say to that, Ryan ran a frustrated hand down his scruffy face. He hadn't shaved in three days, and it probably made him look like a crazy person after being woken up to this mess in the middle of the night.

"I want to believe it was an accident," Josh continued, "because of our history, but honestly, it's been a while since I've hung out with him. People change. I know he saw shit in the Army. Does he have PTSD?"

Ryan nodded. "Yeah. Flashbacks. Nightmares. He sees a shrink once a week, although, in the beginning, it was three times a week. He doesn't take any of the medications they tried because of different side effects, and he said the doc was okay with that. He's been doing better lately, since returning home, but the flashbacks and nightmares are going to be with him for a long time most likely."

"Excessive anger issues?"

"No, absolutely not." He shook his head. "No more than most people. I can tell you he's known Gi since she was little and has been in love with her for a few years, according to him. They only recently started dating though. I can't see him doing this on purpose, but I wasn't there."

"All right. Let's go talk to Regina and get the whole story. But word of warning, I need you to be calm in there —*she* needs you calm. No outbursts. No threats of killing him, no matter how much that urge bubbles to the surface. Got it?"

"Yeah. Got it." Apparently, Josh had become really good at reading people, because as much as he didn't think Buck had hurt Regina intentionally, a part of Ryan still wanted to kill his best friend for hurting her at all.

Josh led the way down the hall, past several rooms with signs above the doors announcing what they were used for—Trauma, Cardiac Care, etcetera. He stopped next to a partially opened door, under the words "Suture Room." Entering first, he closed the door after Ryan stepped in behind him. His sister was lying on her side on a gurney, with her back to them, and a nurse was setting up a tray with instruments on it nearby. A female, uniformed officer stood quietly in the corner, using a stylus to type something into a tablet.

Although he'd been prepared for it, the sight of Regina's back, exposed by the hospital gown she was wearing, was a shock. Red slices of varying degrees of lengths and depths ran from her neck downward, disappearing under a sheet that covered her from her waist down. He didn't know how much further the cuts went, but what he saw was bad enough. He forced down the anger he felt at seeing her hurt like that, remembering what Josh had said about staying calm. "Gi?"

She glanced over her shoulder and burst out crying when she saw him. He rushed around to the other side of the gurney and squatted next to her, brushing her hair from her wet, red face. "Shh. It's going to be okay."

Clutching his arm, she held on tightly. "N-no, it's n-not! They arrested Buck. You have to tell them it was an accident. You have to get him out of jail. P-please, Ryan! Please! It's all my fault! You—" She was close to being hysterical. Her wide, puffy eyes pleaded with him.

"Shh. All right. All right. But first, you have to tell the detective what happened." He gestured to the foot of the bed, where Josh now stood. "This is a friend of ours from high school, Josh Boyd. He needs to hear what happened before he can release Buck. Okay?"

Sobbing, she gulped several times before nodding. "O-okay."

Josh moved to the side of the gurney next to Ryan. "I'm sorry we had to meet this way, Regina, but can you tell me what happened, from the beginning?"

She nodded again and wiped her eyes. "I-I was sleeping in his bed. He'd told me he couldn't fall asleep next to me because of the nightmares. He was—was afraid he might hurt me." She took a shuddering breath and let it out. "After I fell asleep, he went out to the couch in the living room. I woke up, and it was dark out. At first, I didn't know what had awakened me, but then I heard him calling out. He sounded—I don't know . . ." Her gaze shifted between the two men a few times before settling back on Josh's face. "Scared, I guess. I went to the living room and . . . and he was a mess, caught up in the blanket. He looked like he was in pain, thrashing around. He was calling out orders and—"

"Orders? What kind of orders?"

"To his men. Other soldiers. Stuff like, get down and watching out for something—I don't remember what exactly. He yelled for a corpsman, and then he screamed, 'incoming.' That's when I tried to wake him. I-I couldn't watch him like that anymore. I had to wake him up. I tried calling out his name, but it didn't work. I moved closer and touched his shoulder. The next thing I knew I was falling backward onto the table. It broke and cut me up. The noise seemed to finally wake Buck, and he jumped up. He started to panic when he saw me, asking if I was okay. He—he called 9-1-1 right away. They told him not to move me until the medics got there. When the police arrived . . ." She swallowed hard. "They put handcuffs on him and arrested him." Her gaze focused on Josh, pleadingly. "But none of it was his fault. Please, you have to believe me."

The door swung open and a middle-aged man strode in, wearing glasses and dressed in scrubs. "Sorry, gentlemen, but I need to interrupt and ask you to step outside while I tend to the patient." He eyed Regina's back for a moment. "It might take a while to get all the small slivers out and then stitch a few spots."

Ryan squeezed Regina's hand that he didn't remember

taking hold of. "I'll be right outside, Gi. Everything is going to be all right. I promise."

"You'll release Buck?" she asked Josh.

Clearly not willing to commit right then, the detective said, "Let me talk to the arresting officers first. I'll let you know in a little bit."

She nodded again but looked miserable. Ryan gave her hand another squeeze and pasted a terse smile on his face. "I'll come back in when the doctor's done, okay?"

"Okay."

As he followed Josh out of the room, he heard the doctor say, "Ms. Vaughn, I'm Dr. Zweig. Has the pain medication kicked in yet?" She must have said yes or indicated that it had because he continued. "Good. When was your last tetanus shot?"

Ryan didn't hear anything more because the door closed behind him. Leaning against the wall in the hallway, Josh asked, "So, what do you think?"

"She's telling the truth. No doubt in my mind." That, of course, didn't make him feel any better, but the homicidal thoughts he'd been having about Buck had dropped down to beating the crap out of him.

"I agree. Listen, I know this is hard on all of you. PTSD causes a lot of damage on the home front. But I have a suggestion. Not sure if it's been considered before, but would he be averse to getting a support dog? My cousin's husband has PTSD, but his has more to do with being in crowds than nightmares. He got a support dog last year, and Mike says it's the best thing to happen to him besides his wife and kids. The dog is trained to comfort him and lead him out of situations that are stressing him. It's kind of cool to watch.

"I was out with him one day at Home Depot, and the lines were pretty long. I didn't realize what was happening right away, but damn, that dog did. He started nudging Mike away from the others. When I saw Mike's face, I finally realized he'd been on the verge of panicking. The dog got him out of the crowd and off to the side. Mike slid to the floor against the wall and the dog was all over him, licking him and keeping others away from him. After a few minutes, Mike was able to get up and walk outside as if nothing had happened. I paid for the stuff and found him sitting on a bench, back to his old self again. Well, his old, new-normal self. Anyway, if I were you, I'd suggest it to Buck."

Ryan sighed heavily. As angry as he was about Regina's injuries, he knew he couldn't blame Buck. Ryan might not have PTSD to the extent his friend did, but he did suffer from the occasional nightmare that would scare the devil himself. "I'll talk to him about it. In the meantime, are you going to drop the charges against him?"

"Yeah. I'll head to the station now and tell the guys to release him. I'll write it up as a PTSD-related incident, with no intent to harm. He'll be out within the hour."

"Thanks. I'm going to call Justin to go pick him up. Don't release him before that. He's got to be freaking out over this, and I don't want him to be alone and wanting to do something stupid."

"No problem." Josh pulled a business card out of his wallet and handed it to Ryan. "My cell is on the back. If you need anything or want the name of the organization that pairs dogs up with vets, let me know."

Ryan took the card with one hand and extended the other for Josh to shake. "Thanks. I appreciate everything."

The other man smiled. "We Grizzlies have to stick together, right?"

A chuckle escaped him as some of the tension in his body eased. The Largo Ridge High School mascot was a grizzly bear.

Ten minutes later, Ryan disconnected the call he'd made to Justin, waking him up to tell him to go get Buck from the police station. The guy hadn't been thrilled with his phone ringing at 4:00 a.m., especially since it sounded like he had someone else in bed with him. But he'd gotten his ass up in a hurry after Ryan had explained what'd happened.

Assured Buck was taken care of, Ryan leaned against the wall across from the closed door to the suture room and crossed his arms. He had no idea what this was going to do to Buck and Regina's budding romantic relationship, but he hoped they could get past it. He may've been pissed and shocked when Buck had first told him he was dating Gi, but the more he'd thought about it, the more he'd accepted it. After all, if you couldn't trust your best friend with your sister, who could you trust her with?

seventeen

"Thompson, let's go. You're being released."

Sitting on a hard, wooden slab, that was an incomparable version of a bed, in the jail cell he'd been put in over ninety minutes ago, Buck looked up at the uniformed officer who'd arrested him. "Huh?"

He was still dressed in the lounge pants he'd put on after reluctantly slipping out of his own bed, leaving Regina sound asleep. The cops had let him put on a T-shirt, jacket, and work boots, which he'd slid his feet into without socks, before cuffing him and putting him in the back of one of the patrol cars. When they'd put him in the holding cell, they'd had him remove his shoelaces and the cord from the waist of the pants. He'd even known why—so he didn't try to commit suicide. Not that he'd do that. He wasn't that fucking crazy, although he could see how tonight had taken him one step closer to that point. The average rate of veterans committing suicide per day in the US had dropped to seventeen from twenty. That was a number that was still too damn high. The last thing Buck wanted to be was another statistic, but the PTSD he was dealing with had driven many veterans to end it all —permanently.

Using a large, steel key, the man unlocked the cell door and slid it open. "Your girlfriend convinced the detective it was an accident. Said you were having a PTSD flashback and didn't realize it was her."

Yeah, that's exactly what happened, but it didn't make Buck feel any better about it. It was the exact reason he'd told Regina he couldn't sleep with her. Now it was apparent he couldn't even fall asleep with her being in the same house. He'd hurt Regina—badly. His shirt she'd put on had been ripped to shreds—so had the skin on her back, ass, and thighs. He could've killed her. The thought sent a shudder through him.

He must've hesitated too long because the officer said, "C'mon. Let's go. A friend of yours is waiting for you upstairs."

Buck doubted it was Ryan—the guy probably wanted to kill him.

Sighing, he got to his feet and shuffled out of the cell. The officer led him through a wooden door to a room with a desk and a bunch of equipment Buck didn't recognize. On one wall was a height chart. That was probably where they took photos of prisoners. The big machine in one corner looked like it might be a fingerprint scanner with a monitor attached. They hadn't taken his picture or his prints. With the charges being dropped, none of this would show on his record, but he felt the guilt worse than if it had been anyway.

A door opened, and Josh Boyd walked in. They'd run

into each other occasionally over the years and had hung out together now and then, but lately, they hadn't crossed paths much. Josh wasn't smiling at him, but he also wasn't frowning. Instead, there was sympathy in his expression. "How're you doing Buck?"

"Obviously, not well."

The uniformed officer handed him his wallet, jacket, and other stuff, then told him to sign a form confirming he'd received everything they'd taken from him when he'd first arrived at the station.

Once that was all done, Josh said, "I'll take him upstairs, Dan, if you want to finish up and head back out."

The officer glanced at the clock. It was almost five in the morning. "Thanks. Hopefully, the last two hours of the shift will be quiet."

Josh gestured for Buck to follow him to an elevator at the end of a small hallway. When he pushed the call button, the door immediately slid to the right and disappeared into the wall. They rode up one flight in silence, then exited when the door opened again. Josh gently grabbed Buck's elbow and stopped him in his tracks. "Listen, I saw Regina at the hospital. She's going to be fine, and she's more worried about you than she is about herself. I saw Ryan too. He's obviously upset, but he also understands this was completely unintentional on your part. Regina knows she shouldn't have gotten that close to you when you were trapped in whatever nightmare you were having." As the man spoke, Buck couldn't look at him. The sympathy in his voice was hard enough to deal with—Buck couldn't take seeing it in his expression too. "When I talked to Ryan, I told him about my cousin who has PTSD issues. He was able to get a support dog, and it was the best thing he could've done for himself. You should look into getting one."

When Buck just nodded in agreement, not even sure what he was agreeing to because he just wanted to get out of there, Josh continued. "Anyway, Justin's out in the lobby waiting for you. This way."

Buck trailed a few steps behind him until they reached a door leading out into the lobby. Through a small window, he could see Justin sitting on a bench, his head back and his eyes shut. When the door opened, Justin's eyes flew open, and he jumped to his feet, concern written all over his face. "Hey, you okay?"

"Yeah, just get me out of here."

"Sure." His gaze shifted to the man who was now standing behind Buck. "Hey, Josh."

"Hey, man. Good to see you. Thanks for coming down."

"No problem." He looked at Buck again. "Ready?"

"Yeah." He started for the doors leading to the parking lot but then turned around and held his hand out to Josh. "Listen, thanks. I'm sorry we had to see each other like this. I'll look into what you were telling me about."

"Good. I really think a dog might help."

Buck shrugged, his gaze darting around to anything that wasn't the man's face. "We'll see."

"Good luck."

"Thanks."

With Justin at his side, not saying a word, Buck strode out into the early morning air, his shoulders sagging in defeat. Yesterday, he'd been the happiest guy around, with the woman he loved by his side. Now, he was going to have to end things with her. He'd never forgive himself for what'd happened, and he wasn't going to risk it happening again.

※ ※ ※ ※ ※

By Saturday, Regina was miserable . . . and bored out of her mind. She'd been forced into at least a four-day weekend because she hadn't been able to go to work. On top of being doped up on painkillers, she'd been unable to sit for long thanks to the still healing scratches and cuts on her butt and upper thighs. With a few deeper wounds on her back that'd needed stitches, she could only lay on her stomach or her side. Thankfully, those were the ways she was most comfortable when sleeping to begin with.

When her brother had brought her home from the hospital on Thursday morning, it'd been around 7:00 a.m. He'd gotten her settled into bed, where the narcotics, lack of sleep, and adrenaline crash had prevented her from keeping her eyes open. She'd awoken three hours later to find Ryan had picked up her prescription from the pharmacist and had taken the day off work to stay with her. By noon, however, his hovering had driven her crazy. She'd told him if he didn't go to work, she was going to post a few embarrassing photos of him on Facebook and Instagram—like the one of him as a toddler wearing their mom's high heels and makeup.

He'd finally relented, and she'd had the house to herself, at least for a few hours. With the new security cameras at the front and back of the house, and new deadbolts on the doors, she felt safe enough to be alone. Ryan could also check the video feeds throughout the day and would get an alert if any of the doors or windows were breached. Not that he could reach her in time if that happened, but the security company had left a small sign at the end of the driveway, announcing the house was being protected by their service. Hopefully, that would scare away the person who'd been targeting Regina. The police still hadn't come up with a viable suspect.

Her heart was hurting, and not because of what'd happened, but because of the after-effect. She'd been calling and texting Buck, begging him to talk to her, but he'd ignored all of them with the exception of one text. He'd responded, "I'm sorry. I never meant to hurt you."

She'd left voice messages telling him she didn't blame him or hate him. She loved him and wanted to be with him to get past this. Realistically, she knew he was feeling an enormous amount of guilt and couldn't face her, but that didn't help the feelings of abandonment filling her. Unfortunately, she needed another day or two before she was off the drugs and could comfortably sit in the driver's seat of her SUV and go find him. Whether he liked it or not, she wasn't letting him go without a fight. Not now. Not after making love to him. She had to convince him that it'd been an accident—one she'd caused. Not him.

A few of her girlfriends had texted or called to say hi, and Regina had downplayed the reason why she couldn't go out with them over the weekend. Zia was the only one who knew the truth of what had happened. After her initial shock and anger, she'd calmed down. She'd been Regina's sounding board over the past few days and had even volunteered to come home to Largo Ridge to kick Buck's ass for being a butthead. As much as she'd appreciated her friend's offer, Regina knew that wasn't the solution. However, she didn't know what the solution was.

Lying on her side on the living room couch, she pushed and pulled on the pillow she'd had under her head, trying to fluff it up a bit. According to the cable box, it was a little after 4:00 p.m. She'd spent almost the entire day alternating between binge watching a police drama show on Netflix and dozing off for short naps. The painkillers gave her brain fog, and she was going to try and use Tylenol instead of the next prescription dose. The main thing that physically hurt her now was the pull on the stitches whenever she moved. The ER doctor had told her he'd needed to use seventeen stitches to close up three incisions that'd been too deep for Steri-Strips. Ryan had helped her apply an antibiotic ointment to her back, twice a day, while she'd used the bathroom mirror to see and get the stuff on the wounds on her ass and thighs. The last of the Steri-Strips had fallen off that morning. As much as she wanted to take a shower, she'd have to wait for Ryan to come home. The ER nurse had given her clear, plastic shields to tape in place over the stitches, so they wouldn't get wet, and she couldn't reach back to get them on properly.

Her phone rang, and she snatched it from the coffee table, praying it was Buck. Her heart sank when she saw it was Ryan calling. Knowing he'd worry if she didn't answer, she connected the call. "Hi, Ry."

"Hey, Gi. Just calling to check on you. Do you need anything? I'll be on my way home soon."

Did she need anything? Yeah, she needed Buck. "No, I think I'm good. Oh, wait. I finished off the last of the milk. Can you stop and grab some?"

"Sure. How does Chinese sound for dinner? I'll pick it up on the way."

She pondered that for a moment, then said, "That works. Steamed dumplings, a shrimp roll, General Tso's chicken, and orange soda."

A soft chuckle came over the line. "As if you order anything else. See you in a bit."

"Okay."

Disconnecting the call, she hesitated a moment before hitting the speed dial for Buck. When it went to voice mail after only two rings, she sighed and waited for the beep. "Buck, please call me. I hope you're listening to my messages instead of just deleting them. I . . . I just need to see you, to know you're all right and to show you I'm fine too. Please call."

A few tears rolled down her cheeks, and she wiped them away then placed the phone back on the table. Determination flowed through her. Tomorrow, whether he liked it or not, she and Buck were going to have a showdown, and she prayed she was the victor.

eighteen

*R*yan knocked on Buck's office door, entered, and shut it behind him without a word from either of them. With all the work that needed to be done for the ski season and decorating for Halloween—they had two days before the haunted hayrides started—Buck had been able to avoid his best friend. However, it looked like that time was over. Like Regina, Ryan had left Buck some voice and text messages, which he hadn't answered. Yeah, he'd been a chickenshit, wanting to put off the inevitable confrontation as long as possible.

Not taking a seat, Ryan crossed his arms and glared down at Buck from the other side of his desk. Sighing, Buck tossed his pen on the papers he'd been going through, leaned back in his chair, and ran a hand down his face. "You don't know how sorry I am, man. But I guarantee it'll never happen again. I-I—"

"And how the fuck are you going to do that?" Ryan spat out. "By never seeing her again? By being an asshole about the whole thing? She's been crying her eyes out for days, Buck, and not because of what happened, but because you won't answer her calls or messages or go see her. That's what she's hurting about."

He leaned forward again and slammed his hand on his desk. "I can't see her! I can't talk to her! She deserves someone who isn't going to wake up swinging and send her to the fucking hospital!"

"No, she deserves someone who fucking loves her and treats her like she should be treated. You have PTSD, Buck. You're not responsible for things you do in the throes of a flashback or a nightmare. They suck. I get it. I have my own demons from being in those hellholes on the other side of the world, but we each have varying degrees of them and our reactions to them. Gi gets that.

"Yeah, I wanted to kill you the other night, but once I calmed down and she'd explained what'd happened, I knew I couldn't be mad at you. Maybe someone who hasn't seen and done the same things as you wouldn't understand, but I do. And so does Justin. But Gi? She's never gone through any of that. All she wants to do is love you and help you in any way she can. You're my best friend, dude. If I didn't think you and she were good for each other, there's no way I'd be standing here, trying to convince you to suck it up and go see her. You guys can get past this, but only if you fucking try. Avoiding her is not going to make either of you happy, and it's not going to solve things."

Ryan let out an exasperated breath. "Look, when I talked to Josh the other night, he made a good suggestion—"

"The dog," Buck interrupted.

"Exactly. I think it's a great idea. I did some research. Veterans who have support dogs are singing their praises, saying the dogs gave them their lives back. Josh said he could hook you up with the organization that his cousin got a dog from."

"So, then I'll not only have to worry about hurting someone I love if I have a flashback, but also a dog. Great. That makes me feel so much better." The sarcasm in his tone wasn't hard to miss.

Taking a few steps forward, Ryan put his hands on the desk and leaned over, getting in Buck's face. "Putting our friendship aside, you owe Gi, damn it. You owe her an apology for being an ass the past few days. You owe her for running at the first sign of trouble. You owe her because you gave her your love and then took it back because you're too fucking stubborn to see that she's the best thing to ever happen to you. Now, you know how you're going to make it up to her?" Without waiting for an answer, he continued. "You're going to suck it up and go see her. You're going to get down on your fucking knees and apologize for being an asshole. Then you're going to call that organization and ask about getting a dog to help you through the bad times with Gi at your side. Don't make me throw down with you, Buck, because this is one fight I guarantee you won't win."

Buck stared at his friend. Ryan should be kicking his ass right now for hurting Gi both physically and emotionally, but the guy had his back, as he'd always had since they'd been little. Hurting Gi was bad enough, but hurting Ryan on top of that made it so much worse.

He swallowed hard and tears overflowed, streaking

down his face. "I'm sorry, Ry. I'm so fucking sorry. I never meant to hurt her."

As Ryan circled around the desk, Buck stood. They embraced as only two longtime friends could—friends who'd seen each other at their best and worst and still had one another's six. Buck sobbed against Ryan's shoulder, while Ryan slapped his back a few times. After a few moments, Buck gulped, pulled himself together, and took a step back, so he could look his friend in the eye. "I need her, man. I love her."

"I know you do. So, get off your fucking ass and go get her."

✿✿✿✿✿

AROUND TEN A.M. ON SUNDAY, after Ryan had left for work, Gi finished blowing out her hair, then changed into a loose pair of sweatpants and a long-sleeved T-shirt. After applying a little makeup to make her look less like death-warmed-over, she was ready to hunt down Buck and demand he talk to her. If he thought he could just walk out of her life after making her fall in love with him, he'd better think again. He was about to have a come-to-Jesus moment with Regina holding the reins.

She was in the kitchen, searching for her car keys, when the doorbell rang. Her heart leapt, and she prayed it was Buck finally showing his face. Rushing to the door, she yanked it open before checking to see who it was on the other side. Her happy face dropped as she stared at the man standing in front of the storm door.

With a faint smile, Edward said, "Hi, Regina," loud enough for her to hear through the glass.

Shock morphed into a sliver of fear. What in the world was he doing there? He'd never come to Largo Ridge with her when they'd been together—had never been to her childhood home. Her brain shifted to her flat tires and the brick that'd been thrown through the plateglass window. Had he been to Largo Ridge before over the past few weeks and been responsible for the vandalism as a way of getting revenge? She had her cell phone in her hand. Would she have time to dial 9-1-1 if he tried to break in?

When she didn't say anything or open the storm door for him, Edward frowned. "I'm sorry to just show up like this, but I was hoping we could talk. You owe me that much."

Recovering, she asked, "What are you doing here? How did you know where my house was? You've never been here before."

"It was on the wedding guest list for your brother's invite." His mother had insisted on sending Ryan one even though he would've been walking Regina down the aisle. "I just plugged it into the GPS of my rental car. I flew up this morning from the city because I really need to talk to you. Can I come in?"

Still keeping the door between them, she crossed her arms over her chest. "This is the first time you've been here? You didn't come up last week or two weeks ago and vandalize my car and living room window?"

His eyes grew wide. "What? No! Someone damaged your car and house? And you thought it was me? I would never do something like that to you." Hurt flashed across his face. "I thought you knew me better than that."

Actually, she did. There was no way Edward had been behind the vandalism. Dropping her arms, she unlocked the storm door and pushed it open. "I'm sorry, Edward. I know it wasn't you. We just can't figure out who did it and why. Come on in."

Before he could step forward, Ryan's voice came through the speaker attached to the camera next to the front door. "What the fuck are you doing there?"

Startled, Edward backed up. Regina sighed and leaned around the door jamb, putting her face up to the camera lens. "It's fine, Ry. He's just here to talk. No worries."

"You sure?"

She glanced up at Edward. "Yeah, I'm sure."

"K. Call if you need me."

Opening the door wider, she beckoned her ex-fiancé inside. "Sorry about that. He's been in major protective mode the past few weeks."

"It's okay—I completely understand."

"C'mon into the kitchen. Can I get you something to drink?"

He followed her. "Water would be fine, thanks."

While she poured him a glass of water from the five-gallon cooler they used, he glanced around the kitchen. "This place suits you."

Not sure what he meant by that, she didn't respond. Setting the glass on the table, she gestured for him to take a seat, moving to sit opposite him. "What are you doing here, Edward?"

Settled into the chair, he lifted his hand and let it drop.

"Honestly, I don't know. I-I guess I need you to tell me what happened between us. I know you tried to explain after you called off the wedding, but I was too angry and hurt at the time to listen to you."

He looked so lost, so confused, and Regina's heart ached for the man she'd once agreed to marry. "I'm so sorry I ended things the way I did, that I waited so long to do it. Everything just happened so fast. I did love you, Edward, but I don't think I was ever *in* love with you—not the way my parents were in love with each other. But we were so comfortable together, and when you proposed, I guess I thought I was supposed to say yes. I mean, if we'd gotten to that point, it was the next logical step, right?"

Edward nodded. "I can understand that. In fact, honestly, I hadn't wanted to propose to you—not then. Deep down, I didn't think we were ready. Wasn't sure if we ever would be. I loved you too, but like you said, I don't think I was *in* love with you. It was my mother's idea that I propose to you. She wanted to plan a grand affair, and then have us start popping out grandchildren—the next logical step."

She reached across the table and set her hand on his. "I'm sorry I didn't say anything to you sooner. I was just overwhelmed. Every time I turned around, your mother was dragging me to pick out a dress, linen colors, invitations, flowers, and all that other stuff. I never had a chance to figure out if we were doing the right thing or not."

A snort escaped him. "Yeah, Mother is good at overwhelming people and taking over. She did it again after you left."

Her brows furrowing, Regina was puzzled by his statement, then it started to make sense. "With Courtney?"

"Yeah." He sighed. "I'm not in love with her, Regina. I never was. Mother threw us together, thinking she could save face with all her friends. At first, I went along with it all because a part of me wanted to prove to you that you made a mistake, leaving the way you did. But now I see it was the best thing you could've done." The corners of his mouth ticked up in a smirk. "Okay, the second-best thing. The first would have been not saying yes to my proposal to begin with, but we're both at fault there."

"You have to tell Courtney and your mother that you can't go through with the wedding, Edward. You deserve someone you love so passionately that you'd go to the ends of the earth for them, and they would do the same for you. Someone that makes it hurt here," she tapped her chest over her heart, "when they're not by your side. Someone who makes you smile, laugh, and hope that, when the time comes, you die before they do because you never want to live in a world where they don't exist."

Biting his bottom lip, he nodded in agreement. "Definitely not Courtney. And I'm sorry that wasn't you either, Regina. I hate to admit it, but it's the truth."

"I know it is."

He stared at her a moment. "But you've found someone like that for yourself, haven't you?"

Unable to lie, she squeezed his hand. "Yes. I have. I've known him since we were kids but only recently realized we shared something deeper than friendship. You'll find your special lady someday, Edward. You're a great guy. I know your soul mate is out there somewhere, waiting for you to cross her path."

"Thanks. I've decided to start looking for her in California. After I break things off with Courtney, I'm going to put some distance between my folks and me. Mother means well—" When Regina raised her eyebrows at him, he laughed. "Okay, maybe that's not the exact wording for it."

He got to his feet. "I need to get back to the airport. I only wanted a few minutes to talk to you."

Standing, Regina followed him to the front door and out onto the porch. When he turned around and faced her again, she stepped forward and hugged him. His arms tightened around her, and she winced to herself as his hands brushed over her abused back. "You take care of yourself, Regina Vaughn. I hope this guy knows he's snagged one of the greatest women I'll ever know."

She patted his back and moved out of his embrace, smiling as she did. "I hope so too. And I hope you find the right woman for you soon—I know she's out there somewhere." She patted his chest. "Send me a postcard from California when you get there."

"You got it."

nineteen

*A*fter talking with Ryan yesterday, Buck had thought a lot about what his friend had said. He really did owe it to Regina to apologize to her in person and see if they could get past what'd happened. No one was perfect—especially him—and every relationship came with its ups and downs, some worse than others. In the end, hurting her had been a total accident—one he prayed would never happen again.

Instead of going to her house after getting off work the evening before, he'd called his psychiatrist and had a phone session. Dr. Copeland had agreed that Buck getting a support dog might be very helpful. In fact, a good, trained dog would recognize Buck was having a nightmare and could pull him out of it before it got any worse. The psychiatrist had also said that, in time, Buck might actually be able to sleep in the same bed as Regina with the dog on the floor next to him, ready to intervene if Buck needed him. While not completely optimistic that would work, he loved Regina enough to want to try it.

So, he'd called Josh last night and gotten the number for the organization that provided support dogs to veterans. He'd left a voice message on the main number for K9s Kare for Vets and someone had gotten back to him this morning. They'd sent him an email with tons of information and forms that had to be filled out. If they decided he was eligible, the next thing they'd do was interview him about how active he was, where he went most often, and what things he liked to do. That would help them pair him with the ideal dog. He'd actually been excited about the possibility after reading through the paperwork, so he'd printed out the forms and filled them out already. Tomorrow, he'd mail the stack of papers back to the organization, as they'd requested the originals, and keep his fingers crossed he was eligible. Then, he'd have to figure out how to raise the $6000 it would cost him. Training the dog took a lot of work and money, and while it was a nonprofit organization, the donations they received only went so far. Buck had put much of his savings into the down payment on his house, the renovations, and most recently, the furniture he and Gi had ordered. He could ask Grace for an advance on his shareholder check.

For now, he'd take it one step at a time. The first, getting down on his knees and begging Gi for forgiveness.

He was about to pull down her street but slowed his truck and pulled over instead. With his current line of sight, he could see a strange sedan parked in front of her house. But that wasn't what had caught his attention. Regina was standing on the porch with a man Buck recognized from their engagement announcement. "What the fuck?"

Ire filled him as he watched her give Edward Harnett the fucking fourth a long hug. Buck's jaw tightened and his hands clenched the steering wheel so hard his knuckles turned white. What the hell was the guy doing there? Was Regina getting back together with him? They sure seemed cozy together.

As Harnett walked to his car, giving Regina a smile and wave over his shoulder, Buck pulled back into traffic, flooring the accelerator and driving right by the side street. He was fucking pissed. Yes, he'd screwed up—had hurt her physically and emotionally—but it hadn't taken her long to give up on him and go back to the fiancé she'd left at the altar.

Buck smacked his hand on the steering wheel, ignoring the pain. "Should've known it was too fucking good to be true."

With his mind bouncing around with anger, he almost missed the fact he was approaching a red light with cars already stopped ahead of him. Glancing in the rearview mirror, he slammed on the brakes and skidded to a stop a few feet from the car in front of him. The guy in the driver's seat raised his hands in the air in what was probably a what-the-fuck gesture. Buck held up a hand and mouthed, "Sorry."

If he didn't get his head on straight, he'd end up killing someone. As he waited for the light to change, he thought about Regina and Edward—it didn't make sense. From what she'd told him, Harnett had never been to Largo Ridge. She hadn't loved him, or rather, hadn't been *in* love with him. So, what was the guy doing at her house? Wasn't he engaged to someone else now?

The light turned green, and he accelerated just long enough to pull into a gas station and into a spot. He put the truck in park and took a few deep breaths.

You know Gi, asshole. She wouldn't cheat on you. There has to be a logical explanation for Harnett being there, and yet you were ready to think the worst. You're the one screwing up this relationship with her. Don't make another fucking mistake. Go talk to her. Fight for the woman you love.

He should really listen to his inner self more often, instead of acting first and thinking things through later. "All right, Thompson. Go get your girl and don't fuck it up again."

A few minutes later, he pulled into the driveway behind Gi's SUV, effectively blocking her in. After he climbed out of the truck, he looked toward the porch to find Regina standing there with her jacket on and purse and keys in hand. She'd obviously been going somewhere, but not if it was up to him. As he approached, she crossed her arms and cocked her hip. Even with her frown, she was so damn adorable.

"Well, it's about time you showed up."

He climbed the stairs slowly, intently, his gaze never leaving her face, before stopping in front of her. "I'd say it was way past time I showed up." Her eyebrows shot up at his admission. "Want to tell me what your ex-fiancé was doing here before I say something I'm certain I'll regret?"

Her jaw dropped for a moment. "You saw him?"

"Yup." He'd tried to keep the jealous resentment out of his tone but wasn't sure if he'd been successful. He was the one who'd fucked up and was supposed to be apologizing. Starting an argument over something he didn't have the whole story about yet wasn't the way to do that. They had enough problems to iron out between them without him adding any more. But he really needed to know what Harnett had been doing there before he started begging for forgiveness. "What was he doing here?" he repeated.

She inhaled and appeared to be about to lay into him, but then her gaze softened. She set a hand on his arm. "Edward needed some advice, and he wanted to say goodbye. He's breaking his engagement to Courtney and moving to California to make a new start. He forgave me for leaving him the way I did and hoped I was happy with the new man I've started dating. Maybe you know him— he's the guy who can be a stubborn jackass at times."

A snort escaped him. "Yeah, that's an understatement." He glanced down at her purse and keys. "Are you going somewhere, or can we go inside and talk?"

"I was going to look for my stubborn jackass boyfriend and ream him out, but he decided to come here instead and save me the trip."

He grinned at her. With a chuckle and an exasperated shake of her head, she spun around and used her house key to unlock the door. He followed her inside and shut the door behind him. Despite her teasing, he knew he wasn't out of the woods with her yet.

Regina headed for the living room with him on her heels. She took off her coat and tossed it on a wingback chair along with her keys and purse. The chair, with its floral pattern, had been one of the last things her mother had bought before she and her husband had been killed. While it wasn't the most comfortable thing in the world, neither Regina nor her brother seemed to be in any hurry to get rid of it, even though it didn't go with the new couch Ryan had bought last year.

Turning around to face him, Regina crossed her arms and waited. He couldn't read her blank expression, but her body language told him he better start talking fast.

Sighing, he removed his coat and dropped it on top of hers. He held his hands out to his sides, palms up. "I'm sorry, Gi. For everything. For hurting you, not only physically, but for not taking your calls or texts. I was so horrified by what I'd done, I couldn't face you."

Damn it. It was bad enough he'd cried in front of Ryan, but now, his eyes were filling up with tears again. "I promised you I wouldn't run away from you ever again, and the first time shit got bad, I did just that. I was afraid you were going to tell me you couldn't live with my PTSD, and—"

"And it didn't occur to you to ask me if I could live with it? God, men are so fucking dense."

"Humph. Yeah, I guess you could say that." He swallowed hard and wiped his eyes with his fingers before any tears could fall. "Since forgiveness is being given out today, do you think you can toss some my way?"

"You really hurt me, Buck." Not only could he hear the heartache in her tone, but he could see it on her face. "The physical hurt I can get past—that was my fault, not yours. You weren't even aware of what was happening. But I can't keep waiting for the other shoe to drop. I can't live with expecting you to run off every time stuff gets bad or doesn't go according to whatever plan you have in that thick skull of yours."

His heart pounded. Was she saying she wasn't going to take him back? Wasn't going to give him a second chance? "I promise, baby, I may go for a jog or a drive if shit happens, so I can calm down, but I'll always come back to you." He took a step forward, closing the distance between them. Reaching out, he grasped both her hands and brought them to his mouth, kissing her knuckles. "Please, give me another chance. I can't promise I won't fuck up again, but I *can* guarantee I'll do everything in my power to prevent it or make things right again. I'll even get down on my knees, if you want, and beg for mercy."

She studied his face for several moments, leaving him hanging, waiting for an answer. Finally, she said, "I'll forgive you on one condition."

Thank God. "What's that?"

"Ryan said your friend Josh recommended getting a support dog."

A smile spread across his face. "I already filled out the application. They'll let me know in a few days if I'm eligible. It's expensive, but if a dog helps prevent me from hurting you again, I'll sell everything I own to get it."

Tugging her hands out of his, she wrapped her arms around his neck. His hands dropped to her hips and pulled her flush against him. Going up on her toes, she brushed her lips across his. "I forgive you. And I'll do whatever I can to help raise the money for the dog."

"I can't ask—"

"I never said you had to ask. Now, shut up and kiss me."

God, what had he done in his miserable life to deserve this woman? Buck had no idea, but he wasn't going to dwell on it as he kissed her with all the passion he felt. He hoped Ryan wasn't planning on coming home anytime soon, otherwise the guy was going to hear his sister screaming in a way that would probably scar him for life.

Regina pulled away and grabbed Buck's hand, leading him to her bedroom. It'd been ages since he'd stepped foot in the room, and he noticed the changes she'd made to it. It was no longer a teenaged girl's room. Now, the decor made it clear a grown woman lived there.

Kissing, they slowly undressed each other. Buck didn't want to rush this time. It was no longer sex between them. The emotions churning through him told Buck this was what it was like to make love to a woman.

Once they were naked, Buck retrieved a condom from his wallet and tossed it on the nightstand. He sat on the bed, grasped Regina's hips, and pulled her between his legs. When his mouth closed around one of her nipples, her head fell back on her shoulders and her fingers threaded through the strands of his hair, holding his head to her bosom. He laved the turgid peak with his tongue before licking his way over to its mate.

Running his hands over the bare skin of her ass and back, he froze when she tensed and hissed in pain. It took him a moment to realize his fingers had brushed over one set of stitches. Hot guilt rushed through him, and he dropped his hands as if he'd burned her. But Regina grabbed his wrists and brought his hands up to her lower back. "It's okay, Buck. They're just a little sore. Please, don't stop. Make us both forget what happened."

After a moment's hesitation, he kissed the pale skin between her breasts. Now mindful of her injuries, he settled his hands on her waist and lowered himself to lay flat, taking her with him. She straddled his hips, her wet heat resting against his hard length. He lifted his chin and found her mouth again. The little mews coming from her throat spurred him on. His hands and mouth explored every part of her body within their reach, while avoiding the stitches. Her skin was smooth and soft under his calloused palms, which left goose bumps in their wake.

Moving her long hair out of his way, Buck sucked on the sensitive flesh where her shoulder and neck met. Regina's hips rocked back and forth, making him harder than he could ever remember being. His hand searched the bed next to him as she plunged her tongue into his mouth to slide against his. When his fingers finally found what he'd been looking for, he urged her to sit up. She took the foil wrapper from him, opened it, then gently rolled the condom down over his throbbing cock.

Rising on her knees, Regina positioned the tip of his shaft between her legs. Buck fought the compulsion to surge up into her, letting her ease herself down a little at a time. He clutched her hips as her warmth enveloped him. His eyes slammed shut as he tried to gain control.

Finally, she was fully seated on his groin. His cock twitched inside her as she placed her hands on his chest for support. A sexy smile spread across her face as she began to lift her hips before lowering them again. As her wetness eased the glide of his hard flesh against her walls, Buck thrust upward on each of her downstrokes.

Their pace increased as moans and gasps filled the air.

Buck cupped one of Regina's breasts, rolling the nipple between his fingers, as the thumb of his other hand found her clit. She threw her head back and screamed as her orgasm tore through her, her walls rippling around his shaft. Buck's own climax took him by surprise, racing through him as his cries of release joined hers.

Draping herself over his torso, she softly kissed him as they both struggled to bring their breathing under control. He wrapped his arms around her and held her close, not wanting to ever let her go again.

twenty

"That looks beautiful, Tara," Regina praised a little girl, dressed as a fairy, who'd just finished painting a face on her pumpkin. There were a bunch of kids at the ski resort's "Pumpkin Patch Painting" area. Maxi and three members of the housekeeping staff were helping the kids pick out the orange gourds they wanted along with finding the right color paint they swore they needed for their creations. The night before Halloween was always so much fun at LRSR and many of the town's residents came to join the resort's guests in the fun-filled event. A lot of local teenagers also signed up to scare people along the haunted hayride route, which also kept those same teens from participating in what some called Mischief Night. Always the night before Halloween, it usually involved stringing toilet paper in trees, egging cars and houses, and other annoying vandalism. The mayor and town board had expressed their gratitude many times in the past for LRSR keeping the most likely participants in Mischief Night busy with other activities.

In addition to the hayrides and pumpkin patch, there was a scavenger hunt, a costume contest, dancing to a local band, plenty of food to sample, regular and hard apple cider to drink, and games to play. A great time was always had by all.

The last time Regina had volunteered to work the event, she'd been a teenager—actually, it'd been her senior year in high school. She'd been in NY for every Halloween since then, and it was only now that she realized how much she'd missed it. There were some things a city could never duplicate, and a hometown event like that was one of them.

It'd been cold enough all week for them to run the snow-making machines on the slopes, so there was enough packed snow for skiers and snowboarders, and the ice rink had also had some mechanical help in freezing over. Although the slopes and rink were not running during the evening before Halloween, they'd been open earlier and would be available again first thing in the morning. There would be plenty of time for the winter activities in the coming months, so the resort guests never minded missing them for a few hours during special events. From the forecast the local stations had been broadcasting, they'd have natural snow next week with plenty of freezing temperatures. Tonight, it was a comfortable forty-six degrees, which in some areas of the US was either too hot or too cold for this time of the year.

"How's everything going, girls? Do you need

anything?" Grace Scott ambled over to check on them in the smaller of the resort's two pavilions, with concrete floors, wooden roofs, and wooden support beams, that were used for different events throughout the year. The other one currently housed the food, bar, rows of picnic tables, a dance floor, and the band. Grace ran a tight ship every year, and there were rarely any snafus that popped up during the evening.

Grace had opted for a simple witch's outfit this year. In the past, she and her husband had worn some of the most amazing, coordinated costumes, like Cleopatra and Marc Antony or Betsy Ross and Ben Franklin. They'd always kept their costumes a surprise until it was showtime. It must've been hard for Grace to choose something for this year without her beloved Matthew.

"I think we're doing great," Regina responded as she scanned the table full of little ones and their creations.

"Well, the costume contest starts in a little bit." The older woman set a hand atop a little girl's head behind the Minnie Mouse ears she was wearing. "So, hurry up and finish your pumpkins. I expect you all to enter. With these great costumes, it's going to be hard to pick winners."

Regina smiled, remembering Grace had said something similar every year when Regina had been that young.

As they'd been doing all night, screams and roars of laughter erupted from the woods. Tractors were pulling flatbeds topped with hay bales on a wide path through the trees and underbrush. Freddy Kruger, Jason from *Friday the 13th*, zombies, ghosts, vampires, the Blair Witch, skeletons, scary clowns, and others were jumping out from behind trees and large rocks, doing their best to frighten the guests.

While the other women helped the children finish their projects, Regina started cleaning up the paint that was no longer needed, along with the brushes and used paper towels. From behind, large hands grabbed her around the waist just as another round of screams filled the night. She yelped, jumped, and spun around, her heart pounding. Frowning, she smacked Buck on the arm. "Don't do that! You scared the heck out of me!"

Dressed as one of the three musketeers—Ryan and Justin were the other two—he looked so dashing it took her breath away. They'd gotten the outfits at the costume supply place where Grace and Matthew used to get theirs. It catered to theaters and people looking for extravagant getups. The blue cape, hat, and period clothing reminded her of the 1993 film about the musketeers with Charlie Sheen, Kiefer Sutherland, and several other well-known actors. She loved the fact Buck, Justin, and her brother weren't too embarrassed or worried about wrecking their macho images to not go all out with the costumes.

Chuckling, Buck raised an eyebrow. "The 'heck'? That's it?"

"It is when there are little ears around. What are you up to?"

"Just checking on how my little Red Riding Hood is doing," he said with a covert leer, pulling her closer to him. He slid his hands under her red cape and the warmer jacket underneath. She was also wearing a pair of red sweatpants under the skirt of her costume. When it was time for the contest, between the number of people and the heat lamps in the larger pergola, she'd be able to shed the pants and jacket for the contest. "The big, bad wolf hasn't come knocking on your door yet, has it?"

She wrapped her arms around his torso and lowered her voice, making it sexy and suggestive, and for his ears only. "Not yet, but I'm kind of hoping he'll stop by later and eat me."

With an anguished groan, he dipped his head down and gave her a PG-13 kiss, mindful of the big eyes that went with little ears around them.

With a sigh and a shift of his hips, he released her. "I can guarantee you'll get a visit from the wolf later. In the meantime, do you need anything event related?"

"Nope. I don't think so. You're all done with the games?" He'd been assigned to keep the games and parking lot running smoothly, while Ryan was in charge of the hayrides, and Justin kept an eye on the food, drinks, and anything else that wasn't already covered.

"Yeah. Just on my way to the contest." It was the other thing he was running with Grace's help. "You know, next year, we'll have to dress in a couple's theme for the competition."

She smiled. "Sounds good to me. We'll have to find something really good to win."

Leaning down, he gave her a swift kiss. "Let me get going. I'll see you over there."

About ten minutes later, after making certain the last of the children in her care had been returned to their parents, she stood at the far end of the pavilion. Opposite her, at the other end, in front of the band, a small, portable stage had been set up for the contestants to parade across, so those in the back could see them. Different judges were chosen each year, and it was always considered an honor to be selected. Grace kept a running list of past judges, so she could change them each year. No one was allowed to be a judge twice within three years, with most not being picked more than once during a five-year span. This year, the five judges ranged in age from thirteen to eighty-one. The winners would receive a medal and an LRSR certificate pronouncing their accomplishment.

Glancing at the people around her, Regina spotted Renee Miller. The octogenarian was a well-known and well-liked member of the Largo Ridge community, having been the town clerk for over forty years before she'd retired at the age of seventy-eight. When she noticed the older woman shiver, Regina stepped over and squatted down next to her. "Hi, Mrs. Miller. Are you cold? I can run inside and grab a blanket to wrap around you."

Mrs. Miller smiled and cupped Regina's cheek. "Such a sweetheart. Do you mind, dear? The heat lamps don't seem to be penetrating this old, wrinkled skin of mine."

"I don't mind at all. I have plenty of time before the women have to line up." The under-three kids would go first, followed by the four-to-nine-year-olds. Then the ten-through-sixteen-year-olds were next. Seventeen and older put you in the adult categories. The solo men's and women's costumes were judged separately, as were the couples. The final group was the seventy-five and older bunch. It would take about an hour to get through all of them, and the band would provide background music throughout the event.

"All right, everyone, let's get this contest started!" Buck stood on the stage, using one of the band's microphones. "We have some amazing costumes out there this year, and I know it's going to be tough for our judges. Speaking of which, let me hand over the microphone to one of the greatest women I've ever known, LRSR's own Grace Scott, to introduce you to this year's distinguished judges."

As Grace joined him on the stage to a loud round of applause, Regina glanced over her shoulder. It was only a short distance to the main lodge. She'd promised Buck she wouldn't go any place where no one else was around, but with the skeleton crew in the lodge, she wouldn't be alone. Someone was working the front desk and bar, while one of the bellmen would be there too. A few others would be in and out, helping deliver food and drinks to the party. And, of course, there was always someone manning the security office. While there wasn't often a need for security in the family-friendly resort, things occasionally popped up that required them. As for the ski patrol/EMTs, they had their own cabin which was closer to the ski slopes than the lodge, but they were walking around the different event areas in case they were needed anywhere.

Feeling quite safe—especially since nothing bad had happened, vandalism-wise, since the brick through their window—she made the decision to run and get the blanket instead of sending someone else or finding an escort to go with her. It would only take a few moments.

As she hurried toward the lodge, a dozen or so teens and adults were either coming from or going to the building, dressed in all sorts of costumes—mostly ghoulish ones. Those were probably the volunteer staff members from the haunted hayrides. They had an hour break while the contest was in full swing, then they'd have about another hour or two of scaring people again before wrapping it up for the night.

Two women approached her, dressed in seductive outfits. Both had on black, skin-tight pantsuits with knee-high boots, but the blonde had on cat ears attached to a headband and a long tail, while her brunette friend looked like a ninja. They had to be freezing in the thin material but didn't show any signs of hypothermia. When the blonde scowled at Regina as they neared, she recognized her as Margo Shaw. The snobby bitch whispered something to her friend that had the other woman cackling as they passed. Rolling her eyes, Regina shook her head. Some people never outgrew their high school days it seemed.

With her cape flowing behind her, Regina quickly climbed the front steps to the main building and pushed open the door. Warm air enveloped her as she walked through the lobby.

"Hi, Gi. Need something?" Theodora Fisher called from behind the reception desk. At the moment, there were no guests asking for her assistance with anything. There were a few people, some in costume, others just dressed in fall clothing, at the bar or lounging in the sitting areas on either side of a huge, dual-opening, stone fireplace off the lobby.

Regina waved at the thirty-two-year-old redhead. "Hi, Theo. Just grabbing a blanket out of the linen room for Mrs. Miller, if it's okay. It's too cold out there for her."

"Go ahead. That's one of the reasons I volunteered to man the desk tonight."

Regina wondered if one of the other reasons was because Justin was working the event outside. The two of them didn't seem to get along, but Regina thought there was an underlying sexual attraction between them that would rise to the surface some day when they least expected it. They got on each other's nerves a lot, but the air practically crackled whenever they were in the same room—however, it was doubtful either would admit it. It was kind of fun to watch though.

At the far end of the lobby, she climbed the broad staircase instead of taking the elevator. There were sixteen guest rooms on each of the upper three floors, with all the public amenities on the first floor. Recalling that the linen closets for each floor were to the right of the elevators and stairs, she turned in that direction. The first door on her right was a locked maintenance storeroom. The second was the one she wanted, clearly labeled, "Linen Closet," in both English and Braille on a small sign next to the jamb. Turning the handle, Regina was glad to find it unlocked. Opening the door, she found the light switch with her hand and flipped it up. An overhead light came on, illuminating the dark room. There were two housekeeping carts already restocked for tomorrow's duties. To their right was a rolling shelving unit with stacks of sheets, pillowcases, towels, bathmats, and knit blankets.

Keeping the door propped open with her foot, Regina leaned over and snatched one of the blankets. Just as she stood upright again, something came over her head and dropped to her neck before it was yanked backward. Regina's startled yelp was caught in her throat, where it died under the pressure being applied to her neck. She instinctively dropped the blanket and brought both hands up to the piece of fabric choking her —a scarf or something similar. Her back painfully impacted a hard body standing behind her, but the soreness that still lingered from her stitches barely registered in her mind. She struggled to get her hands under the scarf to ease the restrictive force making it difficult for her to breath.

"Fucking bitch," her assailant muttered.

Regina tried to scream, but it came out weak and useless. Involuntary tears rolled down her face. Whoever the man was, he was trying to kill her, and she'd be damned if she'd go down without a fight. She might be smaller than the attacker, but Ryan, Buck, and Justin had taught her how to defend herself after getting their own military training.

Lifting her foot, she rammed it down on what she hoped was his instep. He spat a curse, and her body being swung to the side told her it'd been a direct hit. But she wasn't done yet. She became a flurry of flying limbs, thrusting hips, and a bobbing head. Her elbow connected with a soft abdomen, and she heard a satisfying grunt. It was getting harder to breathe, but she kept up the attack.

Reaching back, her thumb found an eye socket, and she pushed in with all the strength she could muster.

An angry, pain-filled screech hurt her ear, but suddenly, she was free. Ripping the scarf from her neck and tossing it aside, she gulped in lungfuls of air and spun around. Her eyes went wide when she saw who'd attacked her.

Blocking her exit, Marty Sims was covering his right eye with his hand, as he cursed up a storm. He was dressed as a zombie, but she recognized him right away. "You fucking bitch. I lost the resort's account because of you. I'm going to kill you! Do you know how much money I was going to make off this place?"

Without giving him a verbal response or time for him to explain, Regina kicked her foot out, connecting with his groin, sending him flying out into the hallway on his ass. He screamed like a little girl and grabbed his crotch, writhing around in pain on the floor. Sidestepping him, Regina ran to the top of the stairs, her red cape flying behind her. A first attempt to call out to Theodora came out as a raspy squeak, so she rushed down the steps and over to the reception desk. Regina could only imagine what she looked like because the assistant manager's eyes were the size of saucers as she came from around the desk. "Oh my God, Regina! What happened?"

Whispering as loud as she could, because outright talking wasn't happening right then, she told Theodora to call Buck, Ryan, security, and the police, in that order. The other woman picked up the desk phone and a handheld radio at the same time, alerting everyone.

Several guests at the bar and fireplace must have

noticed there was a problem and hurried over. Someone brought a chair and eased Regina into it, while two burly men ran up the stairs to look for her attacker. A kind woman untied the ribbon at Regina's neck, which was holding her cape in place, and let the garment slide down over the back of the chair.

Regina was grateful for everyone's help, but at the moment, she only wanted Buck.

twenty one

The rage racing through Buck's veins had only gone down a few notches since that fucking prick had been taken away in a patrol car. If it hadn't been for all the witnesses, security, and a few other men holding them back, Buck and Ryan would've been the ones being hauled away—for committing homicide. He'd been terrified when Theo had sent a text to his cell phone because he hadn't been able to hear her on his walkie talkie over the band and cheering for the kids in their costumes.

Need you at the front desk, ASAP. It's an emergency!

Somehow, he'd known whatever had happened had involved Regina, especially when he saw Ryan check his phone a few seconds later. After scanning the crowd and not seeing her, dread had almost overwhelmed him as they'd sprinted toward the lodge, with Justin on their heels asking what in the hell was wrong.

Buck had barely beaten the other two men to the lobby, and the relief that'd hit him when he'd seen

Regina alive and sitting in a chair had nearly brought him to his knees. But then he'd noticed her tears and the angry red marks on her neck. He'd been ready to kill someone at that moment, and he hadn't even known who his target was. All Buck knew was the fucker was going to die for even thinking about laying a hand on his woman.

Now, with his arms wrapped around Regina, holding her tightly against his chest, he was reluctant to let her go. Still shaking, she didn't seem to be in a rush to step away from him either. A few uniformed cops and Detective Heath Cobb were still at the scene, interviewing witnesses and collecting evidence. Cobb had assured Buck he'd be charging Sims with attempted murder among other things.

Someone stopped next to Regina and Buck and set a gentle hand on each of their shoulders. "You okay, Gi?" Hogan asked. The tall man was dressed as a pirate, complete with a stuffed parrot on his left shoulder. He'd apparently seen the other men running toward the lodge and had followed to see if they needed help. He'd been one of those who'd kept Buck from killing Sims.

Regina lifted her head and nodded. Her voice was still raspy when she said, "Yes, thank you."

Hogan smiled down at her. "Just checking on you. Bonnie and Clyde would be very upset if something happened to their favorite CPA."

A soft giggle escaped her. "I'm their only CPA."

"True that. But I'm still glad you're okay. Buck, if you need anything, let me know."

Buck's hands remained around Regina's waist.

"Thanks, man. I think we're good. I want to get Gi to the ER to get checked out."

She frowned at him. "I told you, I'm fine. And the medics said that too."

"They also said you should go to the ER and have your throat x-rayed in case there's any crushing injuries we can't see. No arguing, otherwise, I'll sic Grace on you, and you know damn well she'll guilt you into going." The older woman would too. She'd been horrified when she'd learned what had happened inside the resort, but Regina had kept reassuring her that it was nobody's fault except for Sims and, maybe, herself, since she'd gone off without anyone as an escort. As much as Buck wanted to ream her for that, he'd kept his mouth shut. She knew she'd put herself in danger with her stalker still out there—he didn't need to drill it into her head. She was safe now, and that was all that mattered. Hell, he was fucking proud as a damn peacock after hearing how she'd kicked Sims's ass and saved herself.

They were still trying to figure out what Sims had meant when he'd told Regina he'd planned on making a fortune with the resort as his account. Most likely, he'd been plotting to embezzle money from it. Regina and her bosses would have to do an audit, whenever she was well enough to go back to work, to see if Sims had started siphoning money from the resort's accounts before he'd been replaced.

As Hogan stepped away from them, Buck glanced around at all the activity. Justin and Maxine had returned to the pavilion to make sure the costume contest continued and that it kept everyone's attention off the lodge, where several police cars were still parked in the front. Grace and Theo were at the front desk, taking care of the guests and reassuring them it'd been an isolated incident and the attacker had an agenda.

God, he could've lost her.

Leaning down, Buck kissed Regina's forehead. "I'm sorry, Gi."

Her eyes narrowed at him. "For what?"

Where to begin? "You could've been killed tonight. I could've lost you before I ever had a chance to tell you how much I love you."

She cocked her head to the side and winced before saying, "You . . . you love me?"

She doubted him? *Well, you moron, of course she does— you waited this long to tell her.* "Hell, woman, I think I fell in love with you the first time I kissed you. That's one of the reasons I ran from you. I was a fool to wait this long to tell you how I feel."

"Well, I was just as much a fool as you because I think I fell in love with you back then too. I should've chased after you and made you talk to me about why you ran. But in a way, I think you did the right thing, even though it hurt. Things might not have worked out between us if we'd ended up dating then. Maybe they would have." She shrugged. "Who knows? But that's behind us now. And for the record, if I didn't make myself clear, I love you too."

His heart soared. "Thanks for clarifying." He kissed the tip of her nose. "And with our past behind us, we have a future together that I'm very much looking forward to, but first things first—let's go get you checked out and then go home."

She gave him a seductive smile he was thrilled to see because it meant she was thinking about something other than the attack at the moment. Running her palms over his taut chest, she asked, "Any chance I can convince you to just take me home?"

✿ ✿ ✿ ✿ ✿

Three weeks later . . .

"WHAT IF HE doesn't like me?" Buck asked as he followed his truck's GPS directions. They were a mile away from their destination, and he was getting more nervous the closer they got.

"He'll love you, Buck. I mean, what's not to love?" It was the third time Regina had answered that same question with a similar response during the forty-five-minute drive to K9s Kare for Vets. "After getting me to admit I love you, getting a big, fluffy dog to fall for you is a piece of cake."

Their hands were clasped together, and he lifted them to his mouth, kissing her knuckles. "I love you too."

They'd been stunned last week, during the monthly finance meeting with Grace, Justin, Ryan, and Maxine, when his four co-owners told him the resort would be paying for his support dog. Apparently, since K9KV was a nonprofit organization, the cost was considered a donation and was a legal tax write off—not that it'd made a difference to Grace and the others. However, Justin had jokingly blurted out how that fact had swayed his decision to vote in favor of the dog. Buck's extended LRSR family couldn't be more supportive of him getting the assistance dog, and everyone was excited to meet Monty, a big, black, white, and tan Bernese mountain dog.

First, though, Buck had to meet the gentle giant to see if they were as good a fit as the trainers expected them to be. After sending in his application, there'd been numerous emails and phone calls before they'd announced he was an ideal candidate and they believed Monty would be the perfect support animal for him. While he was looking forward to getting the dog—he'd always wanted one as a kid—he wasn't too sure if it would help him with his PTSD. But for Regina, he was willing to do anything that would give him a chance at a normal life with her. One that meant he could sleep in the same bed with her and not worry about hurting her in the middle of the night.

Even though the Largo Ridge ski season had officially opened a few days ago, with just below freezing temperatures, and the snow machines were packing the ski slopes with white fluff, today was Buck's day off. Since the long weekends were the busiest for the lodge, especially Fridays and Mondays with people checking in and out of the resort, Tuesdays and Wednesdays were his free days. Monty wouldn't be going home with him today though—the trainers wanted Buck to come back for two hours a day for the next week, so they could work with him and the dog. Buck needed to learn all of Monty's commands and skills, while Monty had to learn Buck was now his forever human who he needed to take care of. If all went well, the dog would be going home to Buck's house sometime next week.

As for Regina, she was super excited about the dog and told Buck she was taking him shopping on the way home for all the things Monty would need when he arrived at his forever home. He didn't mind though, since he was planning on asking Regina to move in with him as well. He'd talked to Ryan the other night and had gotten his blessing along with two stipulations—one, that Buck never hurt her, and two, that there'd better be an engagement ring coming sometime soon. Buck had no problem with either of those since he'd already started thinking about the ring and when the right time would be to pop the question. While some people might say they were rushing things, Buck knew it had been a long time coming. Now that Regina was his, he wanted to make it legal and binding.

"There's the sign," Regina announced a moment before the GPS's female voice said, "You have arrived at your destination on the left."

Buck slowed down and pulled into the driveway. The first building they came to was a ranch home, but he'd been instructed to go to the long barn just beyond that, which was the training facility.

Giving Regina's hand a final squeeze, Buck let her go, so he could put the truck in park and turn off the engine. "All right, let's do this."

As they climbed from his truck, a door to the barn swung open and a woman in her fifties waved to them. "Hi, you must be Buck and Regina." When they confirmed their identities, the woman held out her hand. "I'm Evelyn O'Shea. It's nice to meet you."

"Nice to meet you too," Regina replied with a huge grin. "To tell you the truth, I think I'm more excited than Buck is. He's a bit nervous."

"About what?"

He shrugged. "Well, I've always liked dogs but never owned one before, so I'll have to get used to that. But I'm more worried the dog won't be able to help me."

A look of comprehension appeared on Evelyn's face. "I understand how you must feel, but you're not the first veteran to worry about that, and I doubt you'll be the last. All I can tell you is with the training, and the close relationship that occurs between the dogs and the veterans they're paired with, we have a ninety-eight percent success rate. We've helped dozens of veterans reclaim parts of their lives that had to be put on hold because of their PTSD symptoms, and that's what we're hoping will happen with you and Monty. Are you ready to meet him?"

"I guess so."

"Good." She opened the door to the barn and gestured for them to proceed in front of her. "Regina, I'm going to ask you to go into our waiting room right over there, while Buck comes with me." She pointed to a door next to a large, plateglass window. "You'll be able to see and hear everything from there, but we find that the initial introduction between the dogs and veterans needs to be without any distractions. Sometimes, we have to remind the family members that these are working dogs first and strict rules must be followed for them to do their jobs."

"Okay, no problem," Regina said as she rubbed a hand across Buck's back. She held up her phone to Evelyn. "Do you mind if I record the introduction?"

"Not at all."

As Regina veered into the waiting room, Buck followed Evelyn into a cavernous space with several training stations and props. No one else was in sight, but he could hear people talking and a few dogs barking behind a door on the far side of the room. Evelyn indicated a bench against one of the walls. "Have a seat there, and I'll bring Monty out. Don't call him over or clap or stand. He's going to sniff a bit until he gets comfortable with you. You'll know when that happens, and then you can talk to him and pet him."

"Okay." Buck took a seat and rubbed his sweating palms against his jean-covered thighs. His heart was pounding in his chest as Evelyn disappeared through the door from where he'd heard the other voices. He glanced over at the plateglass window Regina was standing behind and waved when she gave him a huge smile while holding her phone up to record the coming event.

When the door to his left opened again, Buck's eyes grew wide as a mammoth, furry beast trotted out beside Evelyn. He'd known the dog was going to be big, having researched the breed, but having never seen a Bernese mountain dog in person before, it was a bit of a shock to see the 110-pound male prance about the room. His tongue was lolling out as he heeded several commands the trainer gave him. Evelyn gave him a treat after each proper response, then had Monty heel as she strode toward Buck. The dog's eyes lit up when he spotted the strange man, as if realizing he had a new playmate, and that eased some of Buck's worry as they neared him. Remembering the woman's instructions, Buck sat still and kept his hands in his lap.

Evelyn stopped in front of Buck and ordered Monty to sit. The dog's tail was wagging a mile a minute as he eyed Buck, but he did as he was told. He began to sniff loudly, pulling in the newcomer's scent. Since he didn't growl or seem fearful of Buck, that was a good start—so far, so good.

Without warning, something in the backroom crashed to the floor, echoing in the huge building, followed by someone calling out, "Sorry! Everything's okay!" But Buck's mind didn't register the apology. His body had stiffened as sweat broke out on his brow. He felt the blood drain from his face and tried desperately to swallow the bile that threatened to come up. A ringing started in his ears and quickly became a dull roar. His hands and legs shook, and he was a split second away from bolting.

A heavy weight pressed against his legs, and something wet nudged his hand, pushing under it. Glancing down, Buck saw the big dog had plastered himself against him. Monty began to lick his hands, and the soothing actions had Buck taking large gulps of air as the dog brought him back to the present. After a few moments, Buck reached out and stroked the dog's thick fur.

"Buck, are you okay?" Evelyn asked softly, as she knelt next to Monty without touching Buck. Concern and remorse filled her face. "I'm so sorry. Something was knocked over in the other room. With the high ceilings, everything sounds louder than it should in here."

It took him a moment before he felt he could answer her without his voice cracking. "Yeah, I'm okay." He dropped his gaze to the dog who was still comforting him. "He brought me out of the flashback before it could fully form."

She smiled. "That's what he's supposed to do. I think it was a match made in heaven. Such a good boy, Monty." Letting out a deep, relieved breath, she said, "Why don't we let Monty continue to do his job, while I go get you some water, hmm?"

Kneading the scruff at the dog's neck, Buck just nodded. When the woman walked off, Buck leaned down, rubbed his cheek over Monty's big head, and whispered, "Thank you, buddy."

epilogue

Standing in a room off the vestibule of the small church she'd been baptized in, Regina took the bouquet of flowers Zia handed her. "Thanks."

"You're welcome. And by the way, have I mentioned how gorgeous you look in that dress?"

Regina grinned at her maid of honor. "Only at every fitting and at least three times already today, but thank you again." The simple, ivory A-line style she'd chosen was her ideal wedding dress. It was so pretty, comfortable, and . . . well, it was so *her* . . . and hadn't cost an arm and a leg.

She still couldn't believe she was marrying Buck in less than ten minutes. He'd surprised her at Christmas with an engagement ring, and then begged her not to make him wait too long to hold a wedding. They'd both agreed it was a long time coming, so with the help of those closest to them, they'd managed to plan everything within five months. After the ceremony, they were heading to the ski resort where a huge white tent had been erected and attached to the larger of the two outdoor pavilions. The tent was where the guests would eat, while the band and dance floor were set up under the pavilion.

Buck's mother, sister, and her family had arrived from North Carolina a few days ago, and his nieces, Mia and Hannah, were Regina's flower girls. She'd fallen in love with the six- and seven-year-old imps immediately when they'd first met two months ago, when Regina and Buck had gone south to visit his family. Now, they looked adorable in the pink and purple dresses their mother and Regina had agreed upon.

It had been a great first season for Buck, Ryan, and Justin at the ski resort. Maxi had helped out when she could, as they'd planned, but the men and Grace had done the majority of the work. They'd even come up with some plans for new events and activities to entice their clientele to return for summer vacations.

As for Regina, Grace and the others had convinced her to start her own CPA company and take over the ski resort's account. With Hogan's charity, along with several other business accounts Regina had been able to land, she was already looking to hire another CPA to assist her.

Marty Sims had been found guilty of attempted murder, stalking, and several other charges and would spend, at the very least, the next twenty years in jail. Regina hoped he would rot in there for what he'd done to her. She still freaked out at sudden loud noises, and Buck knew better than to sneak up behind her now. The one and only time he'd done that a few weeks after the assault, with a bouquet of flowers in his hand to surprise her, she'd nearly had a heart attack.

Monty had been a godsend for Buck. Once fully-trained, he'd slowly gained Buck's trust that he'd do what was necessary to help his human through any PTSD episodes that came up—whether Buck was asleep or awake. A month or so after Monty had come to live with them, Buck had spent the first full night in bed with Regina, with the dog sleeping on the floor next to him. Whenever the nightmares came, Monty was on the bed in a heartbeat, lying on top of Buck and calming him down before things got bad. Buck and Regina had slept together every night since.

Monty was also a hit with the staff and guests at the ski resort, walking around in a red vest that declared he was a service dog and asking people not to interact with him while he was on-duty. It'd become a thing, whenever Monty's vest was off for short periods of time, for the staff to announce there was a naked dog in the house who could accept ear scratches, belly rubs, and any Buck-approved treats. LRSR was already planning a fundraiser during the next Halloween week-long event to help other veterans get service dogs.

The door to the vestibule opened, and Ryan stepped in, a broad grin spreading across his handsome face when he spotted Regina. "Almost ready?"

"Yup."

Zia grabbed Mia's and Hannah's hands before leading the girls to the door. "We'll give you a few minutes alone, but don't you dare call me from the highway to tell me to make a godawful announcement this time."

Ryan and Regina laughed before the latter made a cross over her heart. "Not a chance, I swear."

The door shut, leaving the siblings alone. Ryan stepped next to Regina and stared at her in the mirror's reflection. "So, no cold feet this time?"

She shook her head. "Nope, not even lukewarm. In fact, I'm ready to hot-foot it down the aisle."

"I'm happy for you, Gi. Happy you didn't settle, and happy you chose someone I respect and love. Despite my misgivings when you two first started dating, I couldn't have picked a better man for you than Buck."

Sniffling, she waved her hands in front of her face. "Don't make me cry, big brother. My mascara will run."

"Can't have that, now, can we?" He held out his elbow for her to take. "Ready?"

"As I'll ever be."

A few moments later, they were standing at the end of the aisle, watching as the flower girls and Zia made their way to the front of the church. Regina's breath hitched in her chest when she caught sight of Buck standing at the altar, looking more handsome than ever in his black tuxedo. God, she loved him—she always had, even during their time apart when she'd almost made the worst mistake of her life. But now, she knew in her heart that in his arms was where she was supposed to be. With Buck, she'd have the loving marriage her parents had experienced, and it was all she'd ever wanted with the man she loved.

Since Ryan was giving her away, Justin stood next to Buck as his best man. Sitting between them, wearing a white bowtie, was Monty, and Regina couldn't help the giggle that erupted from her at the sight of him.

When the "Wedding March" began, everyone in the

church stood, their eyes tracking Regina as Ryan walked her down the aisle, but her gaze was only focused on Buck's. His eyes sparkled as he stared at her, and she grinned when he crooked his finger at her, indicating he couldn't wait for her to join him.

As they reached the end of the aisle, Ryan handed her off to Buck, who couldn't take his eyes off her. Buck stared at her for a moment before lowering his head and kissing her sweetly on the lips. There were bursts of laughter from their friends and family when the priest cleared his throat and informed them with amusement in his voice, "We're not up to that part of the wedding yet."

Buck smiled against her mouth before ending the kiss. He winked at her and then turned to face the man waiting to wed them. "Well then, let's get this show on the road!"

Other Books by *samantha a. cole*

THE DOMS OF THE COVENANT SERIES

Double Down & Dirty

Entertaining Distraction

Knot a Chance

THE MALONE BROTHERS SERIES

Take the Money and Run

The Devil's Spare Change

THE BLACKHAWK SECURITY SERIES

Tuff Enough

Blood Bound

HAZARD FALLS SERIES

Don't Fight It

Don't Shoot the Messenger

MASTER KEY SERIES

Master Key Resort

LARGO RIDGE SERIES

Cold Feet

AWARD-WINNING STANDALONE BOOKS

The Road to Solace

Scattered Moments in Time: A Collection of Short Stories & More

THE BID ON LOVE SERIES (WITH 7 OTHER AUTHORS!)

Going , Going, Gone: Book 2

THE COLLECTIVE: SEASON TWO (WITH 7 OTHER AUTHORS!)

Angst: Book 7

SPECIAL PROJECTS

First Chapters: Foreplay Volume One

First Chapters: Foreplay Volume Two

First Chapters: Foreplay Volume Three

Word Search For Warriors: Authors For a Cause

Word Search For Warriors: Volume II

Trident Security Coloring Book

Shaded with Love Volume 5: Coloring Book for a Cause

Cooking with Love: Shaded with Love Volume 6

AUTHOR'S NOTE

Any information regarding persons or places has been used with creative literary license so there may be discrepancies between fiction and reality. The missions and personal qualities of members of the military and law enforcement within have been created to enhance the story and, again, may be exaggerated and not coincide with reality.

The author has full respect for the members of the United States military and the varied members of law enforcement and thanks them for their continuing service to making this country as safe and free as possible.

About *samantha a. cole*

USA Today Bestselling Author and Award-Winning Author Samantha A. Cole is a retired policewoman and former paramedic. Using her life experiences and training, she strives to find the perfect mix of suspense and romance for her readers to enjoy.

Her standalone collection of short stories, *Scattered Moments in Time*, won the gold medal in the 2020 Readers' Favorite Awards in the Fiction Anthology genre. Her standalone novel, *The Road to Solace* (formerly *The Friar*), won the silver medal in the 2017 Readers' Favorite Awards in the Contemporary Romance genre.

Samantha has over thirty books published throughout several different series as well has a few standalone novels. A full list can be found on her website listed below.

Sexy Six-Pack's Sirens Group on Facebook
www.samanthacoleauthor.com
Subscribe to my newsletter: eepurl.com/b2hNQj
www.samanthacole.allauthor.com

facebook.com/SamanthaColeAuthor
twitter.com/SamanthaCole222
instagram.com/samanthacoleauthor
pinterest.com/samanthacoleaut

Made in the USA
Middletown, DE
31 October 2021